EL OZ

DAVID DAMIAN FIGUEROA

For Maria "Follow your heart"

ISBN: 978-1-6780-1145-1 (sc)
ISBN: 978-1-6780-1143-7 (hc)
ISBN: 978-1-6780-1135-2 (e)

Library of Congress Control Number: 2022902731

Because of the dynamic nature of the Internet, any web addresses or links contained in this book may have changed since publication and may no longer be valid. The views expressed in this work are solely those of the author and do not necessarily reflect the views of the publisher, and the publisher hereby disclaims any responsibility for them.

Lulu Publishing Services rev. date: 02/16/2022

For Dolores and Pepito

ACKNOWLEDGMENTS

My mother, Antonia, always shared nuggets of her wisdom with me when I was a young boy. She inspired me to follow my heart. I am her loving and grateful son.

Jimmy, you have always believed in me, and I am so grateful for that and you.

I want to express my profound appreciation to Julia Perez for being the best friend anyone could ever ask for while authoring a book. You have taught me the art of listening. I could not have completed *El Oz* without you. To Jackie Pimentel for helping me with edits at the beginning stages. *Mil gracias!*

My deepest gratitude to Alberto Mendoza, and Luis Orozco. Thank you for your guidance and your continuous support.

A special thanks to the National Association of Hispanic Journalists (NAHJ) for your generous grant and for believing in the concept of this endeavor.

I hope you all enjoy the book as much as I loved writing it.

1

El Pueblito de los Milagros

There was a time when El Pueblito de los Milagros was a thriving small town. Life was good, peaceful, and harmonious. Making a living was hard work, but the people were grateful and willing to put in the long hours daily to reap the many rewards from the land.

The annual rains brought showers consistently to the lands near El Pueblito during the last remaining days of summer. The fall temperature was like that of summer, and winters were usually calm during the day and sometimes biting cold at night. But winter was long gone, and springtime was in full force. During the day, the sun shined brightly with an occasional light drizzle of showers in the late afternoon, lasting only a few minutes. Each day's dawn and dusk filled the skies with spectacular colors in layers of yellow, orange, purple, blue, and deep red. Night skies were clear and sprinkled with stars. The moon was so bright at times that you could walk at night and still see the outlines of the trees and mountain ranges.

On a sunny day, the vista's most prominent backdrop was a

dormant volcano called Pico de Orizaba. It had snow on its top throughout the year and was the highest point as far as the eye could see. The fertile volcanic soil working in harmony with ideal weather and water helped grow an abundant harvest season. The vegetables grown in the fields were bountiful. The farmers' yields of *chilmonte, tinda,* chiles serrano, poblanos, corn, tomatoes, onions, and jicama were unmatched. They grew an abundance of pumpkins, melons, oranges, limes, avocados, and peaches. The farmers also grew crops of beans, sugar cane, and alfalfa for feeding the livestock.

La Plaza was the center of El Pueblito, where village society gathered for community events, celebrations, a leisurely walk, or to hear speeches on current affairs. Each day, local merchants sold their wares in the *mercado.* The merchants' trading rivaled their selling, and the shouting of sellers and buyers combined with the crowd's murmur was almost deafening at times. From their *puestos,* the local fishermen sold fish freshly caught in the nearby lake. The farmers sold staple items like vegetables, fruits, bread, grains, tortillas, Talavera poblana, eggs, and dry ground spices. The potters sold ceramic pots to store grains and water. Talavera is hand-thrown pottery shaped and spun from native clay.

The architecture of the buildings in El Pueblito de los Milagros was of the colonial era and was covered in colorful tiles of Talavera and marble. They revealed tall stained-glass windows with Spanish arches and elegant ornamental iron gates at their entrances. The main church was brightly painted with images and carved sculptures of religious and Mayan mythological figures with stern faces. Its main doors were painted in deep cobalt blue that complemented two massive and ornate columns on each side, which seemed too large for the church.

The elders in the community tried to preserve their ancient traditions, cultures, and work ethic. They instilled pride in the youth of their rich heritage but were concerned their traditional living was being tested in ways they could no longer control. The townspeople, villagers, and farmers struggled to adapt and were worried their culture would be lost forever. But life continued moving forward like the wind, with twists and turns.

A giant *supermercado* and manufacturing factory negatively impacted the livelihood of the residents of El Pueblito and the villagers who lived nearby. The greedy conglomerates knew they could hire younger people with fewer skills than the elders, pay them less, and give them long hours to work. The family-owned businesses and mercado merchants simply could not compete with the prices of the new companies. Their customary business model relied on everyone in the family to participate. The farmers were far less productive because they no longer had the younger family members to help with planting and harvesting.

After a year, the local townspeople boycotted the manufacturing factories and the supermercado. They refused to allow their children to work for the greedy operations. With no demand, there was no commerce. So, the business developers closed their doors, and life slowly went back to normal.

Despite their victory, there were still growing concerns. The climate that had been so consistent for hundreds of years began to change. The rains that showered the lands each year were not as constant. Water had become scarce, and the lake's water levels were so low many of the fish died. The elders worked tirelessly, hauling ceramic containers from the nearby lake to water the crops. Still, it was challenging to complete such an arduous task. The townspeople chipped in to help the elders and farmers, but it was not enough.

The traditional family model was once again in jeopardy. The people's endeavor to keep their families united and their small farms financially afloat were failing. More and more young men and women migrated to places like Mexico City and the United States, searching for work to feed their families back home. Life was indeed changing.

2

EL RANCHITO

Outside of El Pueblito de los Milagros lived a nine-year-old girl named Dolores, who had been orphaned as a baby. Her Tia Antonia, her mother's sister, took her in as her own and raised her to be a kind and compassionate child. Dolores loved living with Tia Antonia—affectionately known as Tonia—and her *tios*, Ozvaldo, Wilfredo, Pablo, and Leonardo. The life she lived with them was all she had ever known.

Dolores was relatively small in stature, but like all people who lived in the surrounding area of El Pueblito, she had the same defining indigenous characteristics. Dolores had a small round face and big beautiful brown eyes. The long braids in her hair were interlaced with red and yellow bows and complemented by a freshly picked flower she placed over her left ear. Like Tia Tonia, she wore a traditional sundress with embroidered flowers on its sleeves and huarache sandals.

Tia Tonia was the matriarch of the family. She was kind and soft-spoken. Her calming voice helped maintain peace and harmony within the family, which motivated Dolores to finish her chores and the tios to get their work done on the *ranchito*.

Tio Ozvaldo, Dolores's eldest tio, was adventurous and a natural-born leader. He was tall and wore a mustache. He assumed the role of patriarch in the family and took his responsibilities seriously.

Tio Wilfredo was Dolores's second eldest tio. He was a cheerful dreamer. He had a green thumb for growing plants and was incredibly proud that the vegetables and fruit he grew were free of pesticides. Tio Wilfredo was of medium height, slim, and had shoulder-length hair that parted in the middle at the top of his head. Like most men, he wore suspenders, a long-sleeved shirt, pants made of cotton, and leather boots. He topped off his outfit with a straw hat.

Tio Pablo was the third eldest tio. He was an honest man, but he felt that no one respected him. Like Tio Wilfredo, he was of medium height and had a slim waist. His low self-esteem was evident in his posture. However, once he warmed up to folks, he grew more confident but tended to exaggerate. He took pride in the artisanship he put into his ornamental ironwork, which was proudly displayed on many of the buildings in El Pueblito.

Tio Leonardo was the youngest of the tios. He was a heavyset man with a scruffy beard and was not very tall at all. Although he had a great love for creating hand-thrown Talavera dishes and tile, he felt he was not loved or loveable.

Dolores had not experienced life outside of the family's ranchito. Her best friend was her beloved, loyal, and energetic Chihuahua. The two of them were inseparable. Pepito's white coat with light-brown spots was a blur whenever he chased rabbits that snuck bites of the vegetables from the garden.

Dolores loved learning, but the classes in El Pueblito were too expensive for the family to afford. Tia Tonia decided to give her daily lessons each afternoon in reading, writing, spelling, and arithmetic. Although Dolores enjoyed those subjects, she loved to draw, sing, and practice her *folklorico* dance steps the most.

Dolores and Pepito were early risers. The morning routine was always the same. Each day, the bright morning sun served as an alarm clock by peeking through a small crack in the bedroom window's wooden frame. The bedroom curtains, pillowcases, and bedspread were made from repurposed cotton material of used sacks of flour.

After making the bed, Dolores would line up her handcrafted dolls against her pillow so they could rest for the day. She washed her face in a large bowl, which rested on a pedestal in front of a small hanging mirror. Dolores then combed her hair, changed her clothes, and put her pajamas away in her chest of drawers. Tia Tonia typically made her one egg, one warm tortilla with milk from the cow, and a small glass of orange juice. After eating her breakfast, she fed Pepito.

Dolores and Pepito were always excited to get their day started. They ran out of the house so fast sometimes they would let the screen door slam behind them.

"Slow down—and don't slam the screen door," said Tia Tonia.

Dolores and Pepito immediately slowed their pace.

"Sorry, Tia Tonia," answered Dolores politely.

The morning routine started by making quick stops at different areas of the ranchito to greet each of the tios, who were always already working. The first stop was with Tio Pablo and Tio Ozvaldo, who were welding a decorative iron gate. The tios always gave her a big hug and a tasty treat for Pepito.

Next, they ran to greet Tio Wilfredo, who was hard at work pruning the orange tree. Dolores gave him a big hug, and they darted off to greet Tio Leonardo, who sat on a stool with a spinning potter's wheel making a vase. He petted Pepito on the head and gave Dolores a warm hug.

"Dolores don't forget to do your chores," shouted Tia Tonia.

"Yes, Tia," replied Dolores respectfully.

Dolores and Pepito ran off to complete their chores.

Like most children raised on ranchitos, Dolores was expected to help with daily chores. She helped clean the house, prepare lunch and dinner, pull drinking water up from the well, milked the cow and goat, and fed the pig. Dolores especially liked to feed the chickens near the ramada, which was covered with hundreds of red and orange flowers from the giant bougainvillea tree. They loved to play with the *pollitos*. Pepito had great fun chasing them until the hen became angry and ran him off.

The pollitos were always excited to see Dolores, and she practiced her arithmetic by counting them each day. "Come here, Uno! Come here, Dos! Ven Tres, Cuatro, y Cinco!"

Dolores collected the eggs from the chicken coop in a basket. Some of the eggs would be used for the *desayuno*. The rest would be sold to nearby folks as they made their way down the dirt path to the mercado in El Pueblito.

"Be sure to leave the eggs on the table," said Tia Tonia.

Dolores and Pepito passed the time in the flower garden. They loved chasing the regal monarch butterflies that danced in the air above the bougainvillea blooms, roses, and sunflowers.

Each year, thousands of monarch butterflies made their annual migration from the United States to Mexico. The butterflies laid their eggs, which became caterpillars with green and white stripes. As they matured, they shed their skin, became a chrysalis, attached themselves to leaves of plants and trees, and then covered themselves with silk. In the last process of their transformation, they miraculously turned into butterflies, boasting their heart-shaped wingspans adorned with bloodred, orange, and white markings outlined in black.

"The butterflies are back," whispered Dolores softly to herself. She wondered how the butterflies knew where they were traveling to and when to stop. "Tia Tonia, do the butterflies ever get lost?"

"Dolores, we can learn a lot from the butterflies. They are guided by a higher purpose. They follow their tiny hearts, which serve as an internal compass," replied Tia Tonia.

The sound of bells from Señor Raymundo's rolling cart could be heard from down the path. Dolores and Pepito jumped for joy because they knew he always brought them their favorite, lime-flavored *raspados* and would undoubtedly have unbelievable stories from his travels.

"Greetings, Dolores! Hello, Pepito! It is so good to see you both! I was just in Califas! said El Señor Raymundo. "I'm sorry I cannot offer you a lime-flavored paleta today. The workers are on strike, and they have a lime shortage there."

"That's okay," said Dolores. "Tia Tonia says that we shouldn't always expect to get what we want."

"I have a unique new flavor. It's called strawberry!" replied Señor Raymundo. "I brought it just for you and Pepito. It's the only one that exists in the world!"

"Thank you very much, Señor Raymundo, but what is a strawberry?" asked Dolores.

"Why it's a sweet fruit just like the tuna that grows on the tops of the *nopales!*" Señor Raymundo removed a thick brown cloth to reveal a block of ice. He shaved the ice with a piece of metal into tiny bits. He placed it in a cup, covered it in a sugary syrup made of the tasty fruit, and handed it to Dolores.

Dolores took a careful bite and then offered a taste to Pepito. They both licked their lips vigorously.

Pepito, invigorated by the taste of the strawberry, jumped up and down on his hind legs with joy.

"Strawberry is yummy!" said Dolores. "Califas must be a delightful place to grow such sweet and delicious fruit."

With his kind deed completed for the day, he waved goodbye to Dolores and Pepito.

3

TIO OZVALDO DEPARTS

Dolores and Pepito saw Señora Vicenta, the landlord, on her tiny burro, coming toward them in the distance. Señor Raymundo greeted her as he passed her by, but she snubbed him by turning her face in the opposite direction.

At the beginning of each month, Señora Vicenta paid the family a visit to collect the rent payment for the ranchito. Dolores and Pepito ran as fast as they could back to the house to inform Tia Tonia and the tios of her arrival. On the way back, Dolores stopped at the well to fill a bucket of water for Señora Vicenta's burro.

The family assembled at the front gate entrance and waited for Señora Vicenta to approach. She was a stout woman with a gravelly voice who wore a cloche hat over her disheveled hair. Around her waist hung several timepieces made of silver and gold that she acquired as collateral from local farmers who owed her money for unpaid rents.

"You are behind with your payments!" shouted Señora Vicenta as she dismounted her burro. "Do you have my rent money?"

"Good morning, Señora Vicenta," replied Tio Pablo. "You are correct, but we are only two months behind, Señora."

"One day or one second, you are still late!" replied Señora Vicenta angrily.

Dolores placed the bucket of water near the burro, but Señora Vicenta kicked the pail away, causing the water to spill. The burro continued to drink from the ground, and she smacked him on his behind with a switch to get him to stop drinking. Dolores stepped forward to pet the burro on his forehead to comfort him and make her presence known.

"How dare you hit a defenseless animal?" shouted Dolores. "We may not have any money, like you, Señora, but we have our dreams, and we treat our neighbors with kindness, including the animals! One day we will own this land!"

"You are a disrespectful young lady," replied Señora Vicenta as she remounted the burro. "You can dream if you want, but if your family doesn't come up with the rent soon, I will have you thrown off my land."

Pepito ran over to the burro, looked at him, and winked.

Señora Vicenta took her switch and smacked the burro on its rear. "Let's go!" she shouted.

The burro brayed loudly, kicked his hind legs up, bucked Señora Vicenta into the air, and then took off running. She landed on the dirt, causing a dust cloud, which forced her dress to cover her head and expose her petticoat.

"Señora Vicenta, are you okay?" Tio Leonardo ran to help her get back on her feet, but she pushed him away, dusted herself off, and stormed away, abandoning her burro. When Señora Vicenta reached the top of the hill, she stopped, turned around, and waved her fist at the family angrily in the air. "Remember, I better have the rent soon—or I'm going to have you all evicted!"

Tia Tonia removed the harness from the burro, and Dolores walked him over to the knoll, where he munched on grass contentedly.

"That's enough excitement for one day. Let us get back to our work," said Tia Tonia.

"We need more money," replied Tio Ozvaldo. "I'm going to go and look for work in the City of Angels, and I'm not coming back until I make enough to buy this ranchito from Señora Vicenta."

Unbeknownst to Dolores, the family had fallen on tough times. To make matters worse, the rain showers that fell to the land and nourished its soil before the harvest season had become rare. On the edge of the ranchito was a dirt path that villagers used to make their way to the mercado to sell their goods. A small stream that flowed naturally along the path and into the pond had once been a reliable water source. It helped irrigate the agricultural fields, orchards, and gardens on the ranchito. It had been reduced to a trickle.

Since the pond was nearly empty, the family had to use water sparingly. The abundant crops of fruit and vegetables they sold at the mercado were no longer bountiful as in past harvest seasons. With less to sell, the family had little money to earn. They could barely make ends meet and fell behind in their monthly payments for the ranchito.

Tia Tonia wept at the thought of Tio Ozvaldo leaving the ranchito and her family being separated. She tried desperately to persuade him not to go, but Tio Ozvaldo was determined, fearless, and adventurous. When the reality of the family's financial situation set in, Tia Tonia finally gave him her blessing to leave. She realized that his going to find work was the best thing to do for the family's benefit. So, she and Dolores took the long walk down the winding dirt path to the mercado in El Pueblito. They purchased items they thought Tio Ozvaldo could carry for his long journey through the hot desert and across the border on his way to the City of Angels. They bought a sombrero with a wide brim to block the sun, a jug for water, a satchel to carry food, boots, and a thick wool blanket to keep him warm.

When Tio Ozvaldo first arrived in the City of Angels, he wrote often. Each time a letter arrived, Tia Tonia would kiss the envelope before opening it. Tio Ozvaldo always included a lengthy letter and money to help pay the monthly rent payments for the ranchito. He would also send postcards to Dolores, each with a different photo. Every time one arrived, she and Pepito studied the images from her small collection of postcards of the strange place Tio Ozvaldo now called home.

Several months had passed, and the family had not heard from Tio Ozvaldo. They had not been able to make regular payments to their landlord, Señora Vicenta, and they grew increasingly concerned for his safety and their own dire financial situation.

The family continued to do what they did best, and that was working the land. Like any other day, Tio Wilfredo plowed the fields with the cow. Tio Pablo banged on a piece of iron with a hammer to curve it into shape. Tio Leonardo loaded earthenware into a small wooden cart he planned to sell from his stand at the mercado. Tia Tonia washed clothes with a scrubbing board in an old bathtub out in the yard. Dolores picked the fruit from the nopales' tops using a large stick with a string attached. When a piece of fruit hit the ground, Pepito picked it up with his mouth and put it into her basket.

On this one day, Tia Tonia called Dolores to help hang the laundry on the fence that bordered the property and then left to tend to the rest of the wash. In the middle of her task, she decided to wash her China Poblana dress in a pail of water.

The origins of the traditional China Poblana dress had evolved throughout the decades. They were worn by children for festive holidays. Dolores's dress was beautifully decorated with colorful sequins and beads that sparkled when she twirled in circles. The design pattern had several connecting wings that were almost identical to that of the monarch butterfly.

When Tia Tonia returned to the wash, she was exasperated when she realized Dolores had washed her China Poblana and hung it out to dry.

"Dolores! You washed your beautiful dress?" shouted Tia Tonia. "It's going to shrink!"

"It won't shrink, Tia Tonia." Dolores replied meekly. "I've washed it before." She removed the dress from the clothesline and put it on over her sundress to assure her Tia that it had not been damaged. "See? It still fits." Dolores noticed her Tia was weeping. "Please do not cry, Tia Tonia. I was not trying to ruin my dress. Really, I didn't mean it."

"Oh, *mija*, I'm not mad at you," replied Tia Tonia softly. "We haven't received a letter from your Tio Ozvaldo in such a long time. I'm worried and afraid something awful has happened to him."

The thought of Tio Ozvaldo not returning home was a thought that had never entered Dolores's mind. She was old enough to know that her family's once calm life was changing, and that if there was no work to be had, there would be no money to earn. The possibility of being homeless was now a looming reality. Life was indeed changing for Dolores and her family, but it seemed not for the better. Dolores had an overwhelming sense of concern flow through her body. It was a feeling she had never felt before. "Tia Tonia, are we poor?"

Tia Tonia wiped away the tears from her face. "Dolores, always remember, there is no amount of money or greater wealth than the gift of experiencing life each day." Tia Tonia continued to wipe her tears away. "The time we have right now is the only life worth living."

Dolores felt reassured by Tia Tonia's wise words. They hugged each other and walked back toward the ramada to get lunch and dinner started. A hearty meal made of Tia Tonia's delicious recipes was just what everyone needed to bring their spirits up.

Tia Tonia noticed the dark clouds rolling in over the mountain tops. "I sure hope it rains. We sure need it," she said. "Let's sit under the ramada to prepare the meals."

4

LIKE ANY OTHER DAY

Like any other day, Dolores helped Tia Tonia prepare mouth-watering meals and was tasked to collect all the ingredients in the garden for each recipe. She picked up a big basket for herself and a small basket for Pepito, who was right behind her, ready to assist. They walked past the orchard and headed toward Tio Wilfredo, who was tending to the garden.

Tia Tonia cooked under the ramada shaded by a vast bougain-villea tree with hundreds of orange and magenta blossoms. It was her favorite place to be on the ranchito. She took pieces of chopped wood from the woodpile and placed them in the brick oven. She lit a fire with the wood to heat the cooking grill and the comal for making tortillas.

Dolores and Pepito picked serrano chiles, onions, and toma-tillos for the salsa, and then they continued picking carrots and squash. With their baskets nearly full, they ran back toward the orchard and picked pomegranates, lemons, apples, and peaches. Dolores and Pepito delivered all the ingredients Tia Tonia needed to make the savory meals.

Dolores emptied the baskets onto a big wooden table and broke open each pomegranate.

Tia stirred the pomegranate seeds and walnuts into the bubbling sauce.

Dolores sorted through the pinto beans, removed the dirt clods and tiny rocks, washed them, and soaked them in water to prepare for cooking.

Tia Tonia chopped the vegetables and fruit and heated the comal on the grill to make corn tortillas. Dolores was quite the expert in making tortillas. She would take a small chunk of dough with the tips of her fingers, place it in her palm, and massage the dough into a little round ball with both hands. She used a rolling pin to shape it into a perfect circle. She then clapped the tortilla back and forth with her hands and placed it on the hot comal for cooking. After she completed a small stack, she wrapped them with a cloth, put them into a pottery dish, and covered them with a plate to keep them warm.

Tia Tonia prepared *calabacitas con maize*, queso, dried tomatoes, fresh chopped chiles, and a pitcher of cool lemonade with small fruit chunks for lunch. For dinner, she cooked something more substantial like *Chiles en Nogada*, a dish of stuffed green chiles and fruit with a mouthwatering sauce of pomegranate seeds and walnuts. Delicious frijoles, arroz, tortillas, and salsa were enjoyed with every meal. Still, Tia's *molotes* were scrumptious and the highlight of every meal. They were made with corn masa, stuffed with goat cheese, and served warm.

The enticing aromas of Tia Tonia's cooking carried by the breeze were just as good at summoning the tios for mealtime as any chowtime cowbell. The tios washed their hands with soap in a bucket of water under the ramada while Dolores helped set the table. Tia Tonia lined up all the delicious and steaming hot dishes on a wooden table where everyone served themselves.

The role of saying the prayer before each meal was a tradition and given to Tio Ozvaldo, the eldest son. In his absence, Tio Pablo now assumed that role and led the prayer.

"We are grateful for these gifts we are about to receive. We ask for the protection of Ozvaldo, the safety of our family, and, please, bring us the rain we so desperately need. Amen."

Everyone in the family ate their meal quietly as there was a sense of somberness that clouded the mood. The lack of rain, the rent on the ranchito, and the absence of Tio Ozvaldo were unsettling.

Pepito was not aware of the family's situation and did what dogs usually did. He wagged his tail and waited patiently for Dolores to give him a nibble of her meal.

After lunch was over, Dolores helped clear the table while Tia Tonia washed the dishes in a large round metal tub.

Dolores and Tia Tonia walked back to the house with everything cleaned and put away and sat down on a cot under the porch. Dolores asked Tia to tell her the story of El Mexica people. She never knew if Tia's storytelling would provide delight or cause fright, but whatever the topic, she was always entertained.

"Hundreds of years ago, the El Mexica people evolved and later formalized their culture, which became the Aztecs. They built a sacred civilization around the Great Pyramid of Cholula in honor of their gods and goddesses. They believed the gods had mystical powers over the sun, moon, stars, wind, rain, and more. The people of Cholula experienced a severe drought—just like what we are experiencing now. Just like us, they prayed, but they prayed faithfully to their gods. They made pleas for help from their priests, who ordered them to make offers of the spoiled children. Those children were taken to the top of the pyramid and fed to the gods. Never heard from again."

Dolores and Pepito were scared after hearing Tia Tonia's story and hugged each other for comfort. Dolores was grateful the sun was still out because she was dreadfully afraid of the dark. She got up from the cot and asked for permission to take a stroll by the stream.

Tia Tonia agreed.

Dolores ran up to the clothesline, pulled off her China Poblana dress, and quickly tied it to her waist. She and Pepito ran through the wooden gate at the front of the house and down to the stream.

"Come back soon. It looks like it might rain!" said Tia Tonia.

Dolores looked up at the sky and saw dark clouds rolling in fast, but that did not deter her and Pepito from being adventurous. She liked to stroll down the path along the stream to admire the flowers and trees along the way. They climbed rocks and stared at the trees' reflections on the glistening water. They reminded Dolores of the tall buildings in the postcards Tio Ozvaldo would send from the City of Angels.

They explored until they became tired, and then they lay down under the shade of a tree next to the stream. Pepito rested his weary head on Dolores's lap, and she hummed a song to him. He looked at Dolores lovingly, and they both yawned and fell asleep.

Unbeknownst to Dolores, the family gathered near the ramada, investigated the sky, and observed the large dark clouds
slowly rolling in. They knew these were the signs of stormy weather
ahead. The tios herded the chickens, pigs, cows, and goats into the
port area, where they were kept safely during the storm. The wind
howled loudly, and the trees lost their branches and circled in the
air with the wind's powerful force.

The bougainvillea-covered ramada was propelled midair, and
the earth shook as the sky turned dark red from the dust. Dolores
was frightened and hugged Pepito as tight as she could, but she
lost her grip from the force of the wind. Suddenly, she felt a big
thump on her head and passed out.

"Yes, I'm looking for my little dog. His name is Pepito," replied Dolores. "Have you seen him? I just heard him bark a moment ago."

"I believe I did see your doggy, but first, why don't you give me those feathers—and then I'll tell you where he is?" answered the woman.

"Don't give them to her," sang the flowers nervously.

The woman pointed her cane toward the flowers and yelled, "Shut up—or I'll cut you up into tiny bits of nothing!"

At that moment, Dolores heard a distressed, muffled voice coming from the woman's basket. "I'm in here!"

"Why is there a voice coming from your basket?" asked Dolores.

"Oh, it's nothing. It's just my mischievous parakeet," said the women. "Now, give me those feathers, and then I'll show you where your little mutt is."

"Don't do it. No, don't do it," sang the flowers nervously as they shivered from side to side.

Dolores did not understand the gravity of the situation she was in. "I will give you the feathers if it helps bring my Pepito back." She extended her hand to give the feathers to the woman.

As the woman scooped up the feathers, Dolores noticed she had long claws like a lizard.

The hummingbird flew down and poked her claw with its beak, causing the feathers to float into the air and the top of her basket to open.

Dolores quickly collected the feathers and held them tightly.

"Ouch! You'll pay for that, you rude little mosquito!" The woman made a hissing sound. "You give me those feathers—now!"

Pepito jumped out of the basket and ripped off the woman's cloak. He darted off, but he was stopped by a rope tied around his neck.

The woman's face was uncovered and showed she had eyes like a lizard, scaly skin, and short yellow fangs. She yanked hard on the chain, which tightened around Pepito's neck. "If you don't give me those feathers right now, you'll force me to throw your little mutt into the deep end of the stream—and you'll have to watch him drown."

The hummingbird continued to poke at the cruel woman with its beak.

The woman caught the hummingbird with her claw and squeezed its neck tightly. "Look here, Dolores. I'm giving you one last chance to give me those feathers. Are you really going to force me to throw your mutt in the water and feed this little mosquito to my pet lizard?"

The woman's lizard hissed with excitement.

"No! No! Please don't. I'll give you the feathers, but please don't hurt my doggy or the hummingbird," pleaded Dolores.

The mean woman unhooked Pepito and threw him into the water. She tossed the hummingbird against a tree and then swooped over toward Dolores to take the feathers from her.

Dolores closed her hand tightly as the crazed woman struggled to claw it open. "No! No! No! Somebody, please, help me!" screamed Dolores.

Suddenly, a radiant burst of light with colors of the rainbow shot up to the sky. The flowers clapped their leaves together with excitement and hummed a song.

The cruel woman shrieked with fear and ran down the path to escape.

The light faded, and a beautiful woman appeared holding Pepito, who was sopping wet. She set him down on the dirt path, and he darted toward Dolores for comfort.

The beautiful woman was much taller than Dolores. She had long, black wavy hair and brown skin. Colorful jewels adorned her billowy dress, and she held a glass heart attached to an intricately woven gold rope.

"Hello, my name is Dolores, and this is Pepito," said Dolores, still shivering with fright.

"Dolores and Pepito, I'm Necaxa," replied the woman.

"Why does that cruel woman want the hummingbird feathers so badly?" asked Dolores.

"A long time ago, when my sister and I were young girls, we used to play and make believe we could fly like hummingbirds. Our mother reminded us that we were created to live in the water and sometimes on land. My sister would cry and complain that she felt different. She wanted more, so she spent her time wishing she could fly until a *curandera* visited one day. My sister manipulated the curandera into giving her the recipe for a potion that would grant her wish. She drank it. Over time, her face and hands slowly changed to those of a bird. She sprouted wings, grew claws, and walked out of the water like a bird, but she could only fly for short distances. My sister asked the curandera for help once again. The curandera instructed her to secure the hummingbird's mystical feathers and mix them into the potion to help make her fly. So, now my sister is half fish and half bird—until she can get ahold of the feathers. She wants to rule Ozlandia and being able to fly, which will allow her to continue her destruction."

"I'm sorry about your sister. Who is El Oz?" asked Dolores.

"Thank you, Dolores," replied Necaxa. "El Oz is the leader of Ozlandia."

"I'm lost. I want to go home," said Dolores softly.

In a soft and comforting voice, Necaxa said, "I'm not sure where you live, little one, but Ozlandia is a long distance from here. Follow your heart. It will lead you to El Oz. He's the only one who can help you return home."

"What about Pepito? Can he come with me? I won't leave without him."

"I'm sure Pepito will be welcomed as well," replied Necaxa.

Pepito stood up on his hind legs and clapped his paws with joy.

"Dolores, I must go. You must deliver these feathers to El Oz and not let them out of your sight," said Necaxa.

"Wait! Wait! How do I find El Oz?" replied Dolores.

"Don't worry, little one, just follow your heart. Your heart serves as your internal compass. You'll be fine if you always have the hummingbird feathers with you. They will protect you. Here is something to help you keep them safely until you meet El Oz."

Dolores took the red glass heart and placed it around her neck. She uncorked its top, watched the feathers float into the heart, and then sealed it.

Necaxa slowly vanished into the sky.

Dolores thought, *Follow my heart? How do I do that?*

Dolores was astonished that the dirt path was now covered in the familiar Talavera tiles. She set Pepito down on the tiled path, held the red glass heart around her neck for comfort, and started their journey toward the unknown land of Ozlandia.

La Chaquetza was high above the trees, watching them as they walked away. She rubbed her claws together and salivated as Dolores and Pepito disappeared into the distance. "You'll see, little girl. I'll get those feathers. Los Malalas and I will have you and your stupid mutt for dinner. You'll see."

6

LOS CHIQUITOS

D olores and Pepito were exhausted from walking for such a long time. Dolores pondered Necaxa's words and repeated them to Pepito, "Follow my heart?"

"Yes, that's what that lady said!" answered Pepito.

Dolores was excited that Pepito could speak. "Pepito, you're talking!"

"Is that what I'm doing? I thought I could always speak?" he replied.

Dolores shrugged in acceptance, walked over to Pepito, and picked him up. "Well, Necaxa did say all things are possible here in Ozlandia. I guess it must be true."

They sat down on a wooden stump next to the Talavera path to rest before the long journey to Ozlandia.

"I can't believe we're in this mess of trouble," said Dolores.

"We? You got us into all this trouble!" replied Pepito. "By the way, I am hungry."

"I'm sorry, Pepito. I know you are hungry. I am too, but I am also tired. Let's get some rest and then find something to eat."

Dolores and Pepito leaned on each other, and they both sighed.

"Follow my heart? I'll follow my heart ... when I'm sad and lonely." She looked at Pepito to help with the next set of words.

"I'll follow my heart when it's me only," replied Pepito.

"When I'm feeling discouraged," answered Dolores.

Pepito flexed his front legs with brute confidence and said, "I'll follow my heart when I need courage."

"When I feel a sense of worry ..." replied Dolores.

Pepito scratched his head and looked in the air to help him formulate the next set of words. "I'll be right by your side in a hurry?"

Dolores and Pepito, now in synch, recited the rest of the words to their makeshift poem, "The heart tells you all you need to know and the direction you should go. When you follow your internal compass, there is nothing wrong that can happen among us. The heart does more than thump, thump, thump. It guides you away from life's bump, bump, bumps."

Pepito and Dolores soon fell into a deep sleep.

The hummingbird flew in and hovered over them. It moved in closer to inspect the heart-shaped glass that Necaxa had given Dolores. Satisfied that the feathers were still in safekeeping, it flew away into the sky.

The hummingbird played an essential part in the lives of everyone across the land. It was their protector and had been driven close to extinction by the poisons La Chaquetza sprayed over the crops. The hummingbird watching over Dolores and Pepito was the only one left, and it flew back and forth to Ozlandia to watch over her nest of tiny eggs.

Dolores and Pepito were awakened by loud noises in the distance.

"What are those sounds?" asked Dolores.

"It sounds like music from the ranchito!" replied Pepito.

The sounds moved closer. Clash! Thump! Clash! Thump! Boom! Dolores recognized the style of music and sat up. It sounded just like *banda* music from Sinaloa, where her cousins lived. She realized the drums and rhythmic clashes seemed to be coming closer and closer. Dolores and Pepito could see tiny dancers in the distance as they made their way up the hill. Behind them, the rest of the banda was marching backward. The little musicians were playing *tamboras*, trumpets, tubas, cymbals, cowbells, and tom-toms. They wore red *vaquero* hats on top of their heads and yellow tassels on their long sleeves and the outer lining of their pants.

As they marched by, Pepito and Dolores clapped to the rhythm of the music. They waved at the tiny banda players, but their greetings went ignored.

On the tail end of the banda, a small drum major marched facing the banda with his knees reaching higher with each step. His left hand was placed on his hip, and his right hand waved a glittery baton in the air.

Dolores and Pepito ran up to the banda leader to get his attention. "Excuse me! Excuse me!" shouted Dolores.

The banda leader became infuriated by their interruption and blew his whistle frantically, which made the long hairs of his thick eyebrows fly up. The banda suddenly stopped, and all the instruments went out of tune.

Dolores said, "We're trying to get home back to our ranchito in El Pueblo de Los Milagros. This beautiful lady named Necaxa told us to make our way down this Talavera path to find El Oz."

The banda leader paid no attention to Dolores's desperate plea.

Dolores said, "Necaxa said that the only way I could find my way to Ozlandia was by following my heart, but I don't know how." She dropped her head down to her chest and cried.

Pepito looked at her, and his eyes welled up with tears. He exaggerated his emotions by sobbing uncontrollably. He pointed at Dolores, gave the tiny banda leader a stern look, and said, "You see what you did? You made her cry!"

"I'm sorry, but we're on our way to Ozlandia." The drum major pulled out a long sheet of paper from his coat pocket and showed it to Dolores and Pepito, "Here, read this!"

Pepito moved in closer to inspect the document and read aloud, "It says here that by orders of El Oz, you are to appear in Ozlandia for the coronation of the queen of La Paz."

Dolores replied, "My, that seems like such a tremendous honor. Would you mind if we go to Ozlandia with you? We do not have instruments, but I can sing and dance. And Pepito runs fast."

The little banda leader inspected them up and down and said, "Okay, I guess we'll give you both a try."

"Thank you, kind sir," said Dolores. "Why are you marching in the back of the band? Aren't drum majors supposed to march in the front?"

The little drum major seemed confused by her question.

Pepito stood on his hind legs and waved his paws as if he were leading a marching band.

The little banda leader became irritated once again and said,

"I don't know where you're from, but the drum majors here march from the back of the band. How else would Los Chiquitos be able to hear my whistle and see my direction?"

Pepito whispered, "You, see? More questions like that—and we'll end up on our own!"

The banda leader said, "A long time ago, La Chaquetza cast a spell on the skies. The rains stopped coming, and the sun became hotter. She mixed her evil potions, flew over the lake, and poisoned the waters. Los Chiquitos could not grow much in the community garden because there were hardly any clean waters from the stream. The waters were so important because they helped the seeds grow into plants and kept the hummingbirds alive and thriving.

"Los Chiquitos revered the hummingbirds because they played an essential role in the harvest. They flew from plant to plant and tickled their blooms with their little beaks, signaling them to grow into the fruit and vegetables they were to become. There was a time when a vast population of hummingbirds flew freely throughout the lands. They were dependent on the pure water from the rains that streamed into the crops to help them grow. With the waters poisoned by La Chaquetza, thousands of the tiny protective birds died. Soon there was little food to eat, and there was only one lonely hummingbird left. It tried its best at guarding the community garden—the only untainted land they had left. Most of the ripened food had been left to rot because few of los Chiquitos were left to work the harvest. Many of them had become ill, migrated to other lands, or died.

"La Chaquetza was desperate to get her claws on the hummingbird feathers. If she were successful, she could fly long distances, cast her evil spells throughout the lands, and rule all the people with her evil authority. Los Chiquitos knew the wrongdoings of La Chaquetza and tried with all their might to always keep fresh water for the hummingbird to drink."

The little banda leader blew his whistle, and they marched on to the rhythm of the drums.

Dolores swayed her sparkly dress back and forth, and Pepito mimicked the banda leader as they continued their journey on the Talavera path toward Ozlandia.

7

MEETING WELO

After a few hours of marching, Dolores and Pepito stopped to take a break to drink water from the stream. Although Dolores had fun dancing with Pepito and the marching band, she still had a sense of concern in her heart. She had her doubts that they were on the right course to find their way to Ozlandia. If growing up meant she now had to be worried, then she was fine with staying a nine-year-old girl.

Dolores and Pepito were so thirsty and made loud gulping and slurping sounds.

Dolores investigated the water, saw her reflection, and thought if Tia Tonia were watching, she would believe that Dolores did not mind her manners. She longed to reunite with her tia, tios, and everything she knew back on the ranchito.

She continued to gaze into the reflective waters and could see the ranchito from back home appear. Was it a reflection—or a dream? To be sure, she looked behind her and realized she was not dreaming. The water had risen from the heavy rains on the ranchito, and she could see the tios herding the animals to higher ground. Dolores shifted her eyes to a different section of the water and saw Tia Tonia calling for her from the front porch of the house, "Dolores! Pepito! Come home. It is raining! Where are you?"

Dolores desperately tried to get Tia Tonia's attention and shouted into the water, "I'm trying to find my way home, Tia Tonia! Look! I'm right here! Can you see me? I can see you, Tia Tonia! Look! I'm right here!"

Tia Tonia's image vanished from the water just as quickly as it had appeared.

Dolores was so confused. She held Pepito tight against her chest and burst into tears. Pepito cried right along with her, and she felt gratitude that he could keep her company in this strange new place.

Pepito and Dolores calmed themselves down, collected their emotions, and started walking once again down the Talavera path. They noticed thousands of red strawberries growing in long rows. Dolores knew strawberries were a safe fruit to eat because she and Pepito had tasted their delicious flavor when Señor Raymundo gave her a raspado back at the ranchito. They jumped across the stream to pick the strawberries and stuffed them in their mouths. After a short while, Dolores noticed their bellies getting bigger and bigger, but they continued eating the delicious fruit.

Dolores and Pepito did not realize that La Chaquetza was quietly hovering over them. She sprayed a mist of her sleeping po- tion to get them to fall asleep so she could steal the hummingbird feathers hanging from Dolores's necklace. La Chaquetza became frustrated when she realized the sleeping potion did not take effect immediately.

Dolores and Pepito continued walking down the rows of strawberries and eating. They noticed twelve giant sunflowers swaying peacefully in the light breeze. They looked back down the Talavera path and could barely see Los Chiquitos.

Pepito started to yawn, and soon Dolores began to do the same. Pepito stood on his hind legs, stretched his front legs high to the sky, and said, "I'm sleepy." He smacked his mouth a few times, stretched all four legs, and fell asleep on a small patch of strawberries.

Dolores stretched her arms to her side and replied, "I'm sleepy too." She yawned and lay down next to Pepito.

With no effort at all, they were soon both fast asleep.

La Chaquetza glided in without making a sound and landed on the Talavera path. She walked over to where Dolores and Pepito slept and slowly reached in with her claw to remove the heart-shaped glass from Dolores's neck.

The hummingbird was also keeping watch from high above the trees, and it swiftly flew in and poked La Chaquetza's long beaked nose with such force that it made her cry out in pain.

"You pesky little mosquito bird! I will eat you for dinner! You watch and see!" La Chaquetza shrieked in pain, flew to the top of the trees, and cowered.

The hummingbird flew in to check on Dolores and Pepito, who were both still in a deep sleep. It perched on a single strawberry beside Pepito and Dolores and stood guard, waiting for them to awaken.

After several hours, Dolores woke up in a panic. She thought she was back home for a quick moment, but she quickly realized she was dreaming. Was it a dream within a dream? She touched her face to make sure she was awake and woke up Pepito.

Los Chiquitos were long gone.

When she realized they were by themselves again, Dolores whispered, "Oh no. What are we going to do now?"

They walked toward a rickety wooden fence and noticed a small group of sunflowers huddled together to form one large flower. The sunflowers had faces and began to blink their extraordinarily long eyelashes in sync. Dolores and Pepito walked in for closer look. The sunflowers placed their leaves over their mouths and giggled. They greeted them and sang a beautiful song. They accompanied their singing with music by rubbing their leaves together with such rapid friction that it sounded like violins playing.

Dolores and Pepito were amazed. Their song sounded just like the song they had heard from the flowers and played by the banda. The sunflowers' version was prettier. The sunflowers swayed their long stems while they slowly blinked their big, beautiful eyes.

When the song was finished, Dolores and Pepito clapped their hands.

One of the sunflowers popped up from the middle of the group and announced, "Ladies and gentlemen, presenting the one and only Welo!"

The sunflowers parted in half, swayed their leaves in the air in a synchronized motion, and revealed a tall man. He wore a top hat made of cornhusks and carried a long cane of sugar that resembled a walking stick. The man walked toward Dolores and Pepito with swift confidence. He was made of hundreds of thin intertwined branches and knotted twigs. He wore a multicolored coat that formed a design from hundreds of plant leaves and flower petals. He wore palm fawns for pants.

His shoes were tin coffee cans, and his face and hands were made from hundreds of pinto beans. He had the ends of two chopped-off carrots for eyes, and his teeth were yellow and brown kernels of corn. The man pointed his walking stick in the air, posed with the posture of a great showman, and said, "Ladies and gentlemen, it's great to be here in beautiful *Los Jardines de La Comunidad*! For all the foreigners in the audience, that means the community garden. I am a community garden organizer."

Pepito looked over to Dolores with astonishment. "By gentlemen, does he mean me? I'm just a dog!"

The man began to dance a jig, and Dolores and Pepito danced and clapped their hands. The tall man stopped abruptly, and so did the music. He looked toward the sunflowers and said, "Where's my audience? There are only two people here. You were supposed to announce to the community that I was presenting my show today!"

The sunflowers looked down in shame and then raised their heads in synch, covering their embarrassed faces with their leaves.

The man gave the sunflowers another stern look, and they crouched down further. He turned to Dolores and Pepito, smiled, and said, "I'm so sorry, but they mixed up the dates for my show. What I performed just now was the dress rehearsal." The man looked at the sunflowers, smiled, and said, "I'm sorry,"

The sunflowers peeked out from behind the leaves that covered their faces and gave their brightest blushing smiles. Dolores curt-sied, nervously cleared her throat, and asked, "Why are the sun-flowers afraid of you?"

The man looked distressed, walked over to the sunflowers, and hugged one of them.

They began to play soft music.

"I'm usually a kind person, but lately, there is too much un-certainty in our lives. I'm trying to control my anger and be more patient."

Dolores smiled and said, "Hello, Señor. My name is Dolores, and I come from a ranchito near El Pueblo de Los Milagros. We are lost. My dog, Pepito, and I are trying to make our way to Ozlandia to ask El Oz to help us find our way home."

The man looked at Dolores, took off his hat, and replied, "Nice to meet you. My name is Welo." He had never seen a dog before. "What is your name? What are you?"

Pepito looked at Dolores and then back at Welo. "My name is Pepito. I am not a man. I am a dog. Dolores and I are on our way to Ozlandia."

"Ozlandia?" replied Welo.

"Yes, Ozlandia," answered Dolores.

"Pepito and I are trying to find our way back to my ranchito, and Necaxa told me that if we made our way to Ozlandia, El Oz would help us find our way home."

"Necaxa? You met Necaxa? We could sure use her help in saving our community garden," Welo replied.

"Yes, Necaxa," said Dolores. "She asked Pepito and me to de-liver the hummingbird feathers to El Oz in Ozlandia."

"You have hummingbird feathers?" asked Welo.

"Why, yes, I do." Dolores pulled the rope from around her neck and revealed the red glass heart-shaped container.

Welo's eyes grew with amazement. He looked at Pepito, still not understanding the difference between a person and a dog, and shouted, "The queen of peace is here!" He clapped his hands, snapped his fingers, and began to dance.

The sunflowers, fruit, and vegetables sang along.

Welo took Dolores and Pepito by their hands, locked them into his, and spun in circles.

Dolores was confused by the impromptu celebration. "Excuse me! What are you celebrating?

Welo extended his hands out to her and replied, "You, my darling Dolores! You!"

"I don't understand. You're celebrating me?" said Dolores.

"Don't worry, Dolores. I will accompany you and Pepito to Ozlandia," said Welo. "Dolores, I am a community garden organizer. We used to have an abundant crop each harvest season, but La Chaquetza has been spraying poison on the fruit and vegetables that Los Chiquitos plant each season. They are starving because they cannot grow food. Do you think El Oz can help me? Los Chiquitos are counting on me to resolve this problem."

"Thank you! Thank you! We deeply appreciate it," said Pepito.

"Well, Dolores and Pepito, let us be on our way! I will follow you while you follow your heart to Ozlandia!"

Pepito and Dolores waved goodbye and blew kisses to all the cheerful sunflowers. The trio then skipped their way up the Talavera path toward Ozlandia.

8

La Chaquetza Strikes

The skies turned dark, but the moon lit the way. Thousands of fireflies buzzed throughout the night sky. They resembled little moving stars, and they flew into formation. They spelled out queen of La Paz with their tiny bodies illuminating the sky and then morphed into the shape of a crown.

Dolores, Welo, and Pepito were in awe.

Dolores turned to Welo and asked, "So, tell me, what does a queen do?"

Pepito pointed at himself and asked, "More importantly, what does a loyal subject do?

Welo scratched his head and said, "The news from throughout the land was that El Oz would summon a young Mayan princess to deliver the hummingbird's feathers to Ozlandia and restore peace to his people. The young princess's travels to Ozlandia would be arduous and dangerous, and her faith would be extensively tested. El Oz knew a young girl's actions and courage would set the example his people needed to restore their confidence, not in him, but in themselves. Upon her arrival in Ozlandia, there would be a celebration of her heroism. She would be crowned queen of La Paz. The most important thing is that all of Los Chiquitos would evolve and transform."

Pepito said, "Dolores, I think they do important things like dress up in fancy clothes, take long walks in the garden, eat lots of sweets, and dance at parties all day. And her loyal subject, me, well, I will follow you all day. Speaking of sweets, I'm hungry!"

Dolores and Welo chuckled.

"Eating sweets all day and dancing at parties? I do not think Tia Tonia would approve of the queen's duties. Do you think I could be the queen of La Paz and still live on my ranchito?"

La Chaquetza was perched on the top of a tall tree and listened in on their conversation. She spread her wings with such force and swiftness that the loud clapping sound startled everyone. She flew down to where they stood at such a high speed that she knocked Welo to the ground. She quickly flew straight up and glided back down in a spiral.

Dolores ducked and ran behind a bush for protection.

La Chaquetza glided slowly down to the Talavera path, retracted her big black feathers, and walked toward them as they shivered with fright. "I see you there behind that bush, my sweet little girl, and I also see your cornhusk friend. Did you abandon your little dog? I was looking forward to having him for my supper."

Dolores looked around for Pepito but did not see him.

La Chaquetza mocked Dolores in a nasty mousy voice, "Do you think I could be queen of La Paz and still live on my ranchito?" She leaned in with her claw to touch the heart-shaped glass with the feathers hung from Dolores's neck. "Why don't you give me those feathers, and I'll show you how to return to where you came from?"

Pepito, hidden behind La Chaquetza, became incredibly angry when she terrorized Dolores. He darted toward her, jumped on her chest, and knocked her to the ground. He growled at La Chaquetza, ripped the hood off her head with his teeth, and ran away to take cover with Dolores and Welo. La Chaquetza's face was exposed by the moonlight. "The moonlight!" she shrieked. "You are going to pay for this, you stupid little mutt. I will eat you for dinner. You'll see."

La Chaquetza was weakened by the brightness of the moon. She quickly covered her face with the bottom of her cape.

Pepito he ran toward her and removed the hood from her face again.

La Chaquetza cried out again, reached into her satchel, took out a volcanic rock, and threw it at them.

They scattered in different directions, and the rock exploded into hundreds of droplets of lava, causing the trees, flowers, and plants to scream for help.

Pepito, now frightened, jumped into Dolores's arms.

The fireflies swarmed in and drank up all the droplets of lava.

La Chaquetza struggled to collect herself, covered her face, and screamed as she flew away.

Dolores, Welo, and Pepito huddled together and hugged each other tightly.

"I'm scared," said Pepito in a soft voice.

"Me too," replied Dolores.

"Me three. What is your heart telling you?" said Welo.

"Hearts don't speak, Welo!" whispered Pepito.

"My heart is telling me to keep moving forward," replied Dolores.

Dolores had established herself as the leader with that one remark, and they proceeded to make their way cautiously down the Talavera path. In the distance, they saw the sunrise behind the mountain. It was a burning dark red color.

A sense of gloom overwhelmed the frightened trio as they moved forward toward Ozlandia.

9

MEETING HIERRO

In the far distance, a massive volcano billowed white smoke with bursts of flames from its top. The sun was out, but its usual bright shining rays were masked by a gray haze, which caused the sky to appear red. They walked until they saw a long, tall wall with an even taller building behind it made of what looked like pieces of iron. Dolores thought the building was not attractive at all—not like the ones in El Pueblito de Los Milagros. It was made of rusted steel beams covered in sheets of metal.

As they approached its entrance, they noticed two gigantic copper metal doors. At first glance, the doors looked as though they had been shiny at one time. They had a patina of dingy turquoise and needed polishing.

Pepito looked up and noticed two gigantic door knockers made in the shape of metal hearts.

Dolores saw this as a good omen.

"Welo, you're taller than both of us. Go ahead and knock on the door," said Pepito.

An intimidated Welo looked down at Pepito and said, "You want me to knock?"

Pepito and Dolores nodded, and Welo shivered with fright.

Exasperated by Welo's lack of courage, Pepito said, "Okay, okay, I'll knock! Dolores, lift me up."

Dolores picked up Pepito and positioned him in front of the left door. He reached in with both of his front paws, took the metal heart, and used it to knock on the door several times. Pepito's forceful knocks set off loud piping sounds of melodic whistles, which sounded like the song heard earlier hummed by the flowers and played by the sunflowers and the banda. The piping whistles were so loud that they had to cover their ears.

Just as Pepito was ready to knock again, a little door within the gigantic right door opened at the bottom.

A tiny person walked out and said, "Hello!" The man was about half the size of Pepito. A green welder's helmet covered his eyes. He wore large gloves, and a big gray apron only exposed his little boots.

"Hello!" Dolores said. "We're lost, and we're trying to get to Ozlandia."

The tiny person replied, "Let me check to see if the jefe is here." He closed the little door and shouted, "Jefe, are you here?"

A loud voice in the background responded, "No, I'm not here!"

The tiny person looked at Dolores, Pepito, and Welo. "The jefe isn't here." He slammed the tiny door.

Welo inserted his cane just in time to block the door open.

"Now, wait a minute!" shouted Pepito. "We just heard you talking to your jefe in there."

"Okay! Okay!" replied the tiny person. "Just stay here a moment, and I'll go and check one more time." The tiny person closed the door and quickly returned. "The jefe will see you now. Come right in."

They stepped inside into the dark building, and the tiny man led them through a narrow path surrounded by small mounds and enormous piles of both big and small metal parts. They stopped at the entrance of a beat-up school bus, which had been cut in half.

The tiny man carefully cracked open the door to the school bus and whispered, "They're here to see you, Jefe."

Before they walked in, the jefe called out to them, "Come in! Come in!"

The tiny man opened the door, which quickly fell off its hinges and crash-landed right at their feet. The tiny man, visibly embarrassed, tried with all his might to pick up the door, but with no success.

Dolores, Welo, and Pepito jumped into action, and they moved the door to clear the entrance. One by one, they cautiously entered the school bus.

Welo led the way.

Hundreds of gold and silver trophies were stacked to the top of the school bus's roof and crammed into every nook and cranny. In the middle of the room, a desk was nearly buried by papers. A man jumped out from behind the desk. He was covered with dented hubcaps and wore welder's gloves. He wore a shiny pointed hubcap on top of his head with a leather strap under his chin to hold it into place. His hair was made of thousands of strands of thin swirly strips of recycling metal.

"Hello! This is Dolores and her sweet little dog, Pepito," said Welo.

"Hello. Good afternoon," said Dolores.

Pepito greeted the man with a huge fake smile and said, "I'm hungry!"

"Welcome to my empire! I'm Hierro, and you've already met my loyal assistant, Tiny."

Pepito said, "This looks more like a junkyard or a recycling center than an empire."

"Excuse me?" said Hierro. "As you can see, my outfit is made of the finest designer motor transporter hubcaps. I have a spare one in my warehouse that is even more elegant than this one."

"Jefe, do you want me to go get it?" said Tiny.

Hierro said, "How dare you? You know that I'm saving that one for a special occasion."

Dolores, Welo, and Pepito looked at one another with suspicion. They all knew Hierro was telling a fib.

"I used to deal with precious metals like gold and silver, but I wasn't making enough money. So, I switched to motor transporter parts. As you can see, I am phenomenally successful."

Hierro dreamed of one day being made entirely of shiny and new designer motor transporter hubcaps and becoming a VIP in Ozlandia. Years ago, he had owned a very prosperous recycling center. He employed hundreds of Los Chiquitos to help him dismantle the wrecked motor transporters that were delivered from Ozlandia after they were no longer usable.

They turned them into scraps of metal parts and then recycled them. They removed the salvageable parts and crushed the bodies with an enormous flattener that shredded them into tiny chips of metal.

One day, La Chaquetza appeared at his business and commissioned two massive iron ornamental gates for her castle, which was high atop the volcano. The gates were so immense that it required all of Los Chiquitos days to haul them up the steep and rocky terrain. Once the gates were installed, La Chaquetza kindly offered to make them a feast in her castle.

They entered cheerfully—but soon realized they had been tricked. La Chaquetza locked the gates, imprisoned them, and cast a spell on Los Chiquitos, turning them into Malalas. Under her dictatorship, they were forced to be her servants and carry out her evil deeds throughout the lands.

Without the help of Los Chiquitos, Hierro's company soon began to fail. His recycling center was diminished to a junkyard of old motor transporter parts. With no business and barely able to support himself, he felt defeated and worthless. His self-esteem faded away. To make himself feel more important, he exaggerated his stories, and regretfully, he sometimes lied.

"Mr. Hierro, my doggy and I are trying to get back to our ranchito," said Dolores.

"Where are you from, my dear Dolores?" replied Hierro.

"Our home is near El Pueblito de los Milagros. We are on our way to Ozlandia to seek the help of El Oz."

"I, too, am traveling to Ozlandia. As you can see, my empire is remarkably successful." Hierro pulled a thin, shiny iron rod from the wall of the school bus. "This exquisite scepter I'm holding here is made of pure gold and was specially ordered by El Oz. I intend to deliver it personally."

Pepito walked up to Hierro to inspect his scepter and said, "Excuse me, but you might have mixed up your scepters. Are you sure it's pure gold because this one looks like a painted tire iron?"

Tiny sprinted across the room and tried to cover a metal shelf with several cans of gold and silver paint lined up in a neat row.

Hierro threw his hands in the air and said, "But wouldn't you all agree that it looks just like a real scepter?"

Dolores, Welo, and Pepito responded in unison, "No!"

To further prove his point, Hierro directed the tip of his painted tire iron to the light to admire its sheen. The light bulb hanging from a cord over his desk began to flicker and then turned brighter and brighter. The tire iron created a unique sparkle with radiant lights illuminated at its tip. Suddenly, a big poof of smoke and sparks appeared!

Tiny looked at his boss and said, "Wow, Jefe, you have powers!"

Dolores, Welo, and Pepito were astonished.

Hierro immediately took the credit for the light bulb's spectacle and beamed a prideful face of accomplishment. "I told you that my scepter was special and was specially ordered by El Oz."

Suddenly, there was another big poof of smoke and sparks! The light bulb blew out, and the room went dark.

Tiny sprang into action. He unscrewed the burned-out light bulb, pulled another from atop a shelf, and screwed it into the socket.

There was light again, and Hierro's face turned red with embarrassment. "Well, I was exaggerating a little, okay?" said Hierro.

They all gave him a stern look. Hierro lowered his head with further embarrassment and said, "All right then, you got me. Okay, it really is just an old tire iron I spray-painted gold."

Welo said, "Hierro, telling the truth and being just as you are is perfectly fine. Yes, indeed."

Hierro lowered his head in shame and cried. "I don't like telling lies. I really don't. I lost my mojo, and it affected the business of my recycling center. Recycling is good for everyone and everything. I sometimes exaggerate and tell lies to make everyone believe that I'm successful, but I am not anymore. Do you think El Oz can help me?"

Dolores walked up to Hierro and gave him a big hug. When he began to cry louder, she took his hand and patted it. "The most important place is where you're standing right now. I am sure El Oz thinks you are fine just as you are. I know we do."

"My, you must have a big ego to tell such tall fibs," said Welo.

"I do? What's an ego?" replied Hierro.

"Allow me to explain it like this. When the happy in us turns sad, the ego in us is glad. When the happy in us turns glad, the ego in us gets mad," answered Welo.

Hierro continued to weep.

Dolores said, "There, there, Hierro. I have an idea. Why don't you travel with us to Ozlandia? You can ask El Oz for help with your recycling center. Forgive me for saying, but you seem to have a slight problem with lying. I'm sure El Oz can help you with that too."

"It's worth a try!" said Pepito.

Dolores nodded.

Hierro jumped up and down with excitement and made a loud clickety-clang noise. "Tiny, I need you to watch the empire … I mean the junkyard."

"Sure thing, Jefe. I have it all under control," answered Tiny.

And, with that, they all waved goodbye to Tiny, held hands, and set off up the Talavera path to Ozlandia.

10

MEETING EL LEON

Dolores, Welo, Hierro, and Pepito continued along the Talavera path until they arrived at a grove of trees with small, hanging pumpkins with jack-o'-lantern faces.

For Welo and Hierro, it was a typical sight, but Dolores knew that the pumpkins normally grew in a patch in the family garden back on the ranchito. But she was not on the ranchito. She was in a strange place on her way to an unknown land.

The pumpkins were friendly and greeted them as they made their way down the path.

Welo tipped his hat to them, Hierro waved, and Dolores and Pepito stayed cautiously silent.

Determined to make their way to Ozlandia, the group trudged along through the grove. They were tired from the many hours of walking. Suddenly, they came upon thousands of striped roses in all the colors of the rainbow. The air was fresh, and the flowers smelled heavenly.

They saw a large tent and wagons in the distance and decided to walk closer for a better look. They discovered empty wagons with vertical bars that looked like cages. At the entrance an old sign at the yellow and red striped tent spelled out "La Carpa Maravilla." High atop the tent a tattered flag flapped in the wind. They heard a meow, like a small cat, but they could not tell where it came from.

Welo said, "This looks like an abandoned traveling show."

They heard the meow again—only louder this time.

A voice from behind the tent whispered, "Help me. Help me."

They walked behind the tent and found a sizeable tan-colored cat squeezed into a cage too grossly small for his physique. The large cat panted frantically with its long tongue sticking clear out of its big head. "Please help me. I'm awfully thirsty."

For Welo and Hierro, this also was a regular sight, but Dolores and Pepito had never seen a cat that size. Indeed, it was an extraordinary place they were in.

"Hello, I'm Dolores—and this is Welo, Hierro, and my doggy, Pepito. Excuse me, but why are you here all alone?"

El Leon meowed and said, "A few days ago, the performers rehearsed outside of the tent. The animals were out for their meals when an old woman with large black wings flew in with hundreds of winged horny toads. The old woman dropped black rocks from the sky that exploded into fire, and the winged horny toads swooped in and captured everyone, including our ringmaster. I, along with all the other animals, were left here in cages. The chimpanzee retrieved the key to set us all free. She unlocked our cages one by one, but when she was about to open my mine, a group of winged creatures flew in and caught her and the other animals— and they escaped into the skies. I haven't seen them since."

Dolores noticed the key on the ground just outside El Leon's cage and unlocked him. She found a bucket and ran to get water from the stream.

El Leon was sluggish from having sat so long and gradually stepped out. He could barely walk from sitting in the same position for so long.

Dolores sat next to him and stroked his mane for a good long while.

Welo asked, "How did you get to be a part of this carpa show?"

"It's a long story. It all started when I was just a cub," answered El Leon.

El Leon's original owner was El Capitan Melchor, a voyager who sailed the seas to faraway lands searching for gold, silver, spices, and silk. During one of his trips to the west coast of Africa, he went on a hunting expedition and encountered a baby lion that was only a few months old. His mother had been killed by hunters, and the baby lion had been abandoned by the pride. El Capitan knew the baby lion had no chance of survival in the wild, so he kept him for his own and named him El Leon. He never learned to roar because he needed other lions to teach him. He only meowed like a small cat.

As they sailed on to other seas, El Leon became a trusted companion to El Capitan and took him everywhere he went. On one expedition, El Capitan docked his ship on the coast of France. The people were mesmerized to see such a large cat—the likes of which no European had ever seen. News of El Leon traveled throughout the city and people flocked in to get a glimpse of the large, but gentle feline. El Leon loved all the attention and affection he received from the public.

One day, El Capitan received an invitation from the king and queen of France to stay at their castle. El Leon was invited to join him. The royals wanted a firsthand look at the large cat from the faraway land of Africa. The queen took a great liking to El Leon, and she invited him to dine at the same table with the king and other court royals.

The queen commissioned a painting of herself with El Leon at her side. She grew to love El Leon and had her courtiers pamper him. Her lady-in-waiting would dab him with her most pleasing and expensive perfume. Her royal hairdresser combed his mane into a high-powdered hairdo with ribbons and flowers to match hers.

News continued to spread, and other royal courts commissioned portraits of their own. El Capitan and El Leon traveled to all the capitals of the kingdoms of Europe as guests of royalty. El Leon loved every minute of the high life.

After their extended royal tour, they set off for Mexico. During their voyage, the crew encountered a violent storm. El Capitan was swept from the ship's deck and vanished into the turbulent waters. He was never heard from again. The captain's young nephew, who was left in command, took the ship's helm and sailed on to Mexico. When the skies cleared, El Leon looked over the railing and out into the vast ocean with great sadness. He hoped that he would one day see El Capitan again.

When they docked in Mexico, the young ship captain met one of Los Chiquitos, a ringmaster of a traveling tent show called La Carpa Maravilla. The young captain was delighted and amazed by the clowns, acrobats, and Mexican dances accompanied by musicians who played traditional songs.

The performers' costumes were embroidered and had shiny sequins that sparkled throughout the tent's top when the light hit them. La Carpa Maravilla also had a petting zoo of exotic animals for the public. The animals were corralled in a large open space, including a peacock, a chimpanzee, a panda bear, a llama, and a pigmy elephant.

The young captain loved the show and liked the little ringmaster. He witnessed firsthand how happy the animals were. So, he thought it was an excellent place for El Leon to live. The young captain always felt a ship was no place for a lion.

If the captain had investigated closer, he would have learned the ringmaster was not a kind man at all. In fact, he treated all the performers and animals very poorly. When the captain left, the ringmaster put El Leon in a small cage that he could barely move around in. He spent his days and nights sitting up because he could not lie down. He became distressed and meowed through-out the day. El Leon longed for the days when he had his freedom and was loved by El Capitan.

"I see you're a cat—an enormous cat at that—but what kind of cat are you?" asked Welo.

"I'm a lion," answered El Leon.

Dolores placed the bucket of water at El Leon's paws so he could drink.

"You're a lion?" asked Dolores. "Why, Pepito and I have never seen a lion before. You have a meow just like the cat back at my ranchito."

"Yes, I have a meow," replied El Leon. "I was told that I was supposed to roar when I got older, but I never had anyone to teach me how. I have no real voice, and no one loves me." He put his paws over his eyes, wept, and cried out, "Nobody loves me."

Dolores said, "Why, that's not true. It does not matter to me if you can't roar. I love you."

After Welo and Hierro nodded, Pepito put his paws in the air in exasperation and finally agreed.

Welo said, "You, see? And anyone who thinks you are too old to do something a younger lion can only do has antiquated thinking." He walked over to El Leon and began to sing. "When life is taking its toll, you can always sing because singing is like medicine for the soul."

El Leon stood up slowly and replied, "I've been here, and I've been there, but now, no one gives a care."

"Not true, because we love you," replied Dolores.

"I've been neglected and rejected," said El Leon.

Pepito walked over to El Leon and jumped on his back. "But now you're protected!" Pepito gave him a big hug.

"I don't even have a roar—and not by choice," added El Leon.

Welo shouted, "Why don't you come with us to see if El Oz will give you back your roar! Your voice!"

Hierro walked over to El Leon and said, "Even though you meow, I will still bow."

Embarrassed, El Leon looked at Dolores and said, "Really? You are my friends—and you love me? I can travel with you to Ozlandia? I would truly and absolutely love that."

El Leon's spirits were lifted by the encouragement of the group. After a while, he even got his energy back. He stretched his legs, and the four of them, along with Pepito in tow, sauntered hand in hand down the Talavera path to Ozlandia.

11

THE LAKE

In the far distance, they saw a volcano billowing white smoke from its top. On the right side of the volcano was a ledge with a castle on top of it. It was dusk, and Dolores, Welo, Hierro, El Leon, and Pepito continued along the Talavera path.

The path ended abruptly at the edge of a vast lake covered in large lily pads. On top of the lily pads were several monarch butterflies, which were slightly taller than Dolores. At the edge of the lake, a large frog was sitting on a lily pad.

"Hello, Mr. Frog," said Pepito.

The frog made a ribbit sound and then a grunt. "Hello!"

"Hello, my name is Pepito, and this is Dolores. These are our new friends, Welo, Hierro, and El Leon. What is your name?"

The frog made a croaking sound and answered, "Mr. Frog is fine."

"Is there another way to cross the lake?" asked Dolores.

"Unfortunately, there is not. The last person who tried to cross nearly drowned," replied Mr. Frog. "I, like all of the frogs here, used to be one of the Los Chiquitos. There was a bridge on this very spot that hundreds of Los Chiquitos crossed. La Chaquetza set it ablaze with her fire rocks to block any food or supplies from getting to Ozlandia. So, we built small boats and gave rides to travelers. One day, she saw that we were still able to cross the lake, and she cast a spell on us and turned us into frogs."

The group looked to their right and then to the left but could not see the lake's end in either direction. They looked across to the opposite end of the lake and noticed the Talavera path continued from there. Dolores concluded the only way to reach Ozlandia was by crossing the lake by walking on top of the giant lily pads, which were not very sturdy. Welo came up with an idea.

"Pepito, you are the lightest in weight. Why don't you go first?" said Welo.

Pepito began to shiver at the thought that he might drown. He was afraid of the water after his encounter with the evil La Chaquetza. He looked up to Dolores for reassurance and said, "Okay, but please don't leave me."

Dolores picked up Pepito, hugged him, and looked directly into his eyes. "I won't ever leave you. I promise."

Pepito walked cautiously to the edge of the water and placed his right paw on a lily pad to test if it would hold his weight. It did, and he jumped on. He continued to walk until he was about a quarter of the way across the lake.

Then, without warning, they felt the earth shake. The volcano shot a massive explosion of smoke into the air, causing several bolts of lightning to light up the sky. The monarch butterflies were spooked and flew away. The earth shook so hard it caused angry waves of water.

Pepito struggled with all his might to keep his balance, but he was slammed into the turbulent waters. He barked repeatedly and then screamed, "Dolores, please help me! I'm afraid!"

Dolores panicked at the sight of Pepito's desperation and cried out, "Pepito! Pepito!"

Pepito knew how to paddle with his paws, but the water was much too violent. He tried his best to keep his head above the water, and he cried, "Dolores!"

As Pepito sank into the water, Dolores jumped on top of the nearest lily pad and fought to keep her balance as she made her way toward him. She hopped carefully from one lily pad to another until she found Pepito. He was struggling to keep his head afloat. Dolores tried desperately to save him, but she too fell into the water. She swam over to Pepito and grabbed onto him. They both tried desperately to keep their heads above the water.

Welo, Hierro, and El Leon held each other tightly from the safety of the lake's edge.

The frog croaked out, "Are you gentlemen going to help them? I thought they were your friends."

"Water makes me terrified. Can we wait for the low tide?" replied Welo with a look of shame on his face.

"I'm afraid my hubcaps will get rusty," answered Hierro shamefully.

"My mane will get matted, knotted, and wet. If only I had a hairnet," added El Leon with a guilty grin on his face.

In the middle of the lake, the water spun and formed a massive whirlpool. Dolores and Pepito were caught up in the force of the spiraling water and were pulled under again.

Mr. Frog grew overly concerned and let out loud croaks, rib-bits, peeps, clucks, and grunts, signaling for the other frogs in the lake to jump in and help. Mr. Frog directed Welo to climb on his back, but he did not.

Hierro and El Leon shivered with fear.

Two other frogs started jumping from one lily pad to another with rapid speed. When they reached the whirlpool, they struggled not to get sucked under. Mr. Frog directed the two frogs to dive into the vortex to rescue Dolores and Pepito.

Suddenly, the water came to a standstill.

Welo, Hierro, and El Leon looked at each other with dread.

Welo said, "If only I hadn't been so petrified."

"If only I hadn't been scared stiff as steel," said a mortified Hierro.

"If only I hadn't been a fraidy-cat." El Leon covered his guilty eyes with his paws.

They investigated the water and saw small air bubbles reaching the surface. Larger bubbles began to float to the top, and Mr. Frog popped up through the surface along with the two other frogs. They all gasped for air.

Welo, Hierro, and El Leon helped them onto the large lily pad.

Dolores and Pepito popped up right after them.

"Some friends you are," said Pepito as he and Dolores gasped for air.

Dolores thought about how she and Pepito might not have survived and how her Tia Tonia and tios might never see them again. In a soft voice, she said, "Thank you, Mr. Frog. You and your friends saved our lives. How will we ever be able to repay you?"

"When you see El Oz, please ask him to remove La Chaquetza's spell. We long for the days when we were all Chiquitos," answered Mr. Frog.

"I promise I will." Dolores kissed him on his forehead. "Can you give us a ride to the end of the lake?"

Mr. Frog agreed and directed the other frogs to help. Dolores, Pepito, Welo, Hierro, and El Leon rode on their backs to the edge on the opposite end. The frogs hopped onto the Talavera path, and one by one, they all jumped off.

Dolores hugged Mr. Frog and said, "I will never forget you, Mr. Frog. I will keep my promise."

Dolores picked up Pepito and noticed the Talavera path led a winding route up to the volcano. She and Pepito walked to the top of the hill and then looked back at Welo, Hierro, and El Leon with disappointment. The cowardly group bowed their heads with shame. They were no longer feeling welcome or reassured.

Dolores took five more steps and then looked back again. "We're going to Ozlandia. Are you coming?"

Welo, Hierro, and El Leon ran to catch up with Dolores and Pepito. They all hugged and then trudged their way up the steep Talavera path.

12

THE DARK QUEENDOM

Dolores, Welo, Hierro, El Leon, and Pepito continued up the winding Talavera path into La Chaquetza's dark queendom. The air was still, and the billowing smoke from the volcano clouded the sky. In the distance, they saw her castle through the murky atmosphere.

Pumpkins lined both sides of the Talavera path and lit the way to the castle. The pumpkins were illuminated by flickering candlelight inside each of the carved-out evil faces.

The Talavera path ended at the front doors of the castle.

Pepito looked through a space at the bottom of the doors and could see that the course continued to the other side. Pepito began to shake, and his teeth chattered uncontrollably.

The others peeked through and saw a group of Los Malalas jumping in a circle around a large pot of boiling water, which sat atop a raging fire. One of Los Malalas hissed loudly while it stirred the pot's contents with a large wooden spoon.

A group of Los Chiquitos was tied to a large stone column with thick vines. La Chaquetza heckled them from her throne from high above. One of Los Chiquitos cried out and begged for mercy, but La Chaquetza shouted, "There's not a soul that can hear you!"

Los Malalas hissed and flapped their wings and continued circling the cooking pot, anxiously awaiting their meal.

Pepito whispered, "I'm scared. I hope your heart doesn't tell you to go through those doors." He pointed his right-hand index finger and blocked the view with his left hand so only Dolores could see he was referring to Hierro, Welo, and El Leon. "You know we can't count on these three to help us."

"It looks like that's the only way," replied Dolores. "We have to move forward. Otherwise, we'll never make it home."

It took all five of them to push open the heavy doors. The thick smoke allowed them to walk through unnoticed, but the smokey air irritated Pepito's snout—and he let out a loud sneeze that alerted all the Malalas.

La Chaquetza rubbed her hands back and forth and said, "Don't be alarmed, little travelers. You are just in time for dinner. Your little mutt will make a delicious stew."

She ordered Los Malalas to retrieve the shivering group.

Dolores, Pepito, Welo, Hierro, and El Leon ran away as fast as they could. When they reached the edge of the cliff, Los Malalas closed in on them. At that moment, a gust of wind pushed giant floating dandelions to the side of the cliff.

Welo jumped up, grabbed the stem of one of the dandelions, and floated away.

Hierro and El Leon followed right behind. Welo gave an encouraging shout to Dolores, and they both jumped. Dolores grasped the dandelion stem with her right hand and caught Pepito with her left hand—but she struggled to pull him up.

Los Malalas chased them into the air and began to pluck the cottony plumes from the flowers, which caused them to float erratically through the sky. Los Malalas had to retreat because their wings only allowed them to fly only short distances.

It was not long before the group was in the clear. They flew over fields and through valleys, and they landed near the Talavera path along the stream. They walked upstream until they reached the edge of the mesa. A volcano in the distance was shooting lava into the sky. There was no other way to go, and Dolores had an intuitive feeling in her heart like that of the monarch butterfly that motivated her to keep moving forward. Determined now more than ever, she said, "Let's keep going."

As they moved forward, the volcano collapsed within, causing explosions, and pushing smoke and ash to engulf the skies. The clouds thundered with bolts of lightning that vibrated the earth. A fine soot covered their bodies except for their eyes. The intense gray clouds bumped into one another, causing more thunder and rain to pour down.

After a while, the sun filled the sky. Dolores had one thing on her mind—staying on the path—and they picked up the pace and headed toward Ozlandia.

13

OZLANDIA

Dolores, Welo, Hierro, El Leon, and Pepito felt more optimistic, and they danced and sung their way up the Talavera path.

One of Los Chiquitos approached, tipped his hat, and said, "Welcome to Ozlandia! I am El Empresario."

Dolores said, "Thank you. This is Welo, Hierro, El Leon, and Pepito. I'm Dolores."

Pepito saluted El Empresario and bowed.

El Empresario looked at Dolores and said, "Do you have the feathers?"

Dolores was astonished that he knew that she was guarding the feathers. "Yes, I do," she replied hesitantly. She removed her shawl and showed him the red glass heart with the feathers inside.

El Empresario's eyes grew large with excitement, and he extended his hand out to touch the glass heart. At that moment, the hummingbird soared down and hovered right in front of El Empresario's face. He rubbed the top of the hummingbird's head affectionately with the tip of his finger.

Dolores was relieved to see her tiny protector. "Señor Empresario, you know the hummingbird?"

"The hummingbird is my friend, my dear. Her name is Ixchel," replied El Empresario.

Dolores extended her right index finger, and Ixchel flew over and perched. She raised her finger to her face to get a good look at Ixchel. They locked eyes. "Ixchel, thank you for your protection and for helping us find our way." She looked at El Empresario. "Señor Empresario, I know Tia Tonia and my tios must be looking for Pepito and me. We must return home."

El Empresario said, "I'll take you to El Oz, and we'll get you home safely. I promise. In fact, he'll help us all return home."

As they entered the village, there were *puestos* very much like the ones from the mercado in the village back home. Each of the puestos had lines filled with families of Chiquitos huddled together. Each puesto had a sign with different Mexican cities, including Dos Pilas, Rio Bec, Maya, Palenque, and Tikal. Dolores knew those cities, but they were far away from her ranchito. "Why are Los Chiquitos leaving?" asked Dolores.

"It's time for the great migration, my dear. We do this every year!" answered El Empresario.

"What is a migration?" asked Dolores.

"I think it's what we've been doing all along," answered Pepito.

"They are going back to where we came from," continued El Empresario.

"Why did they leave in the first place?" asked Dolores. "We certainly didn't want to leave our home."

El Empresario said, "Dolores, they are securing passes for their trip back home. They are doing what comes naturally to them. It's part of the cycle of life."

"So, they are working toward a better life in their homeland? Like what Tio Ozvaldo is doing by traveling to the City of Angels?"

Pepito said, "Exactly, Dolores. I get it! I understand what is happening now! They are following their hearts."

El Empresario, Dolores, Pepito, Welo, Hierro, and El Leon continued up the Talavera path along the canal bank's edge and saw hundreds of colorful canoes filled with Los Chiquitos. Everyone was cheerful and joyous.

The canoes were filled with musicians, ladies selling flowers, children pushing handcrafted toys in carts, and women making tortillas and tacos. The crowd's murmur reminded Dolores of the mercado from her village.

Pepito's eyes filled with excitement, and he licked his lips and rubbed his little belly from hunger. A *remero* extended his oar and helped them board a canoe, and they headed up the canal toward Ozlandia. The hundreds of casitas, where Los Chiquitos lived, were painted in assorted colors, and everyone waved at Dolores as they floated by.

"Are they waving at me?" asked Dolores.

"They are! They are!" answered Welo.

A small gathering of Los Chiquitos pointed at Dolores. Two little women jumped up and down with joy at the sight of seeing her. As they continued up the canal, Los Chiquitos cheered loudly—and some even threw flowers.

When they approached the dock, a large cheering crowd was there to meet them. "The queen of La Paz is here!"

Dolores recognized the marching band, which was playing the now-familiar tune from earlier in their journey. The group swayed from side to side to the beat of the music.

El Empresario said, "Dolores, it's almost time for you to meet El Oz."

Dolores felt the need to speak on behalf of Welo, Hierro, and El Leon. It was the least she could do since they had kept their promise of escorting her on the treacherous journey to Ozlandia. Each of them had requests for El Oz as well. "But what about our friends here? Welo? Hierro? El Leon?" Dolores pointed to each of them individually. "They have been our loyal friends and protectors just like Ixchel. Welo would like to ask El Oz for help in saving his community garden. You see, La Chaquetza has been spraying poison on the fruit and vegetables that Los Chiquitos plant each season. They are starving because they cannot grow food."

"That's terrible," replied El Empresario. "What about Hierro?"

"Well, Hierro has lost his confidence, and it affected his business. You see, he sometimes tells lies, and he wants to stop that behavior." Dolores looked at Hierro to get his approval. "Did I get that right, Hierro?"

Hierro nodded and smiled. "Yes, Dolores."

"And, what about El Leon?" asked El Empresario.

"El Leon was mistreated by his owner and feels that no one loves him. I love him with all my heart, but I do not think he believes me. Señor Empresario, I'd like to ask El Oz if he could make El Leon feel loved."

El Leon cried uncontrollably.

Dolores walked over and hugged him. "Did I get that right, El Leon?"

Welo, Hierro, and Pepito circled El Leon and embraced him.

"You see, you're a big cuddly cat," said Pepito.

"We love you—and that's all you need to know!" added Dolores.

El Empresario said, "I'm sure El Oz will grant your wishes and help each of you return to where you came from. Tomorrow, I will take you to El Oz. We will let him know that you and Pepito wish to return home, Welo would like to save his community, Hierro wants his confidence back, and El Leon would like to be loved. Did I get that right?"

The group nodded.

"Okay, then it's settled," said El Empresario.

They followed the Talavera path to their casitas, and they hugged one another before they turned in for a night's sleep.

"Good night, Welo, Hierro, and El Leon," said Dolores.

Pepito let out a huge yawn and said, "Good night, everybody."

"Good night, Dolores" said Pepito.

"Good night, Pepito," answered Dolores.

14

MEETING EL OZ

When morning arrived, the bright sun peeked through a sliver of space between the wooden slats of the bedroom shutters. Dolores jumped out of bed, and for a moment, she thought she was in her bedroom back home.

She hunched over, feeling defeated, crawled back under the covers, and hugged Pepito. She stared out the window and thought about how good it would feel to be back home in her own bed. She heard Pepito's belly growl, and they both laughed.

Dolores and Pepito walked outside their casita and found Welo, Hierro, and El Leon having breakfast with El Empresario.

"Please join us, Dolores and Pepito," said El Empresario.

Dolores approached the table and sat down, "I don't think I can eat anything. I'm too excited."

"I'm hungry. What's for breakfast?" asked Pepito.

"You're always hungry, Pepito," replied El Leon.

When breakfast was over, they walked down the Talavera path toward the canal and boarded a canoe to make their way to El Oz. After quite some time, a gigantic pyramid appeared in the distance. The pyramid reminded Dolores of the one her family had visited the year before.

As they approached, they heard loud beating drums and rattles. To their great surprise, the Talavera path continued ahead.

El Empresario began to perspire and appeared hesitant to continue.

"Is something wrong?" asked Dolores.

"The last time I heard those drumbeats and rattles were when we were overtaken by La Chaquetza and Los Malalas," replied El Empresario.

"I think we should turn back and try to meet El Oz on another day," said El Leon.

"No! We're going to move forward," replied Dolores.

"Is your heart telling you to move forward, Dolores?" asked Welo.

Dolores said, "Yes, La Chaquetza wants the hummingbird feathers—and we need them to get home!"

They held hands and proceeded down the winding Talavera path and then up an incline. When they reached the top, they saw the entire pyramid. El Empresario's instincts were correct. La Chaquetza and Los Malalas were in full force. At the center of a platform, toward the middle of the pyramid, stood a little boy. He was about the same age as Dolores. He wore a regal Mayan outfit, which indicated that he was someone of importance.

El Oz led Ozlandia with something more potent than mystical powers. He was just and treated the Los Chiquitos with respect, kindness, compassion, truth, and fairness. And, for that and more, they respected him as their leader. El Oz knew that this was the only way to guide and empower his people to be the same toward others. He knew a united and peaceful people held the power to do good by all and for all.

The evil La Chaquetza held the boy hostage. His hands were bound, and his arms were extended by ropes tied to two large columns. The deafening sound of drumbeats and rattles on the ankles of Los Malalas pounded inside Dolores's chest.

Los Chiquitos arrived soon after and stood behind the group in solidarity.

La Chaquetza immediately noticed them. "My sweet little girl, Dolores. How thoughtful of you to come and deliver the hummingbird feathers."

Dolores replied, "These feathers were a gift from Ixchel. Necaxa told me to never let them go!"

Ixchel flew in, landed on Dolores's shoulder, and whispered into her ear.

Dolores whispered, "I promise. I will do that, Ixchel."

At that moment, there was a flash of light—and Necaxa appeared from the canal's waters. Mr. Frog was with her—and so were all the other frogs from the lake.

Necaxa's apparition caused quite a spectacle of radiance. She walked toward the large crowd that had assembled and said, "Dear sister, you never learned any of the lessons our mother tried to teach you. She always saw the good in you—and I still do too."

La Chaquetza shouted, "Stay out of this! This has nothing to do with you."

Necaxa said, "You are so confused, my dear sister. What you want only for yourself affects each one of us as well. We all want what you want, but the hummingbird feathers that Dolores kept safely are not only for you. They are meant for all of us. We all want to fly. We all deserve to fly home."

La Chaquetza walked over to Dolores and said, "Give me those feathers, Dolores. Don't you see how much trouble you're causing everyone?"

Dolores stared at La Chaquetza for a good long while and then answered, "Okay, I'll give them to you."

Everyone in the crowd, including Los Malalas, gasped loudly.

"Dolores, what are you doing?" asked Pepito.

"Pepito, my heart is telling me to do this for La Chaquetza. She wants to fly. I want to help her, and I shall."

There was complete silence in the crowd as Dolores took the red heart-shaped glass from her neck. She struggled to pull off its top, but Ixchel flew down to help. She pulled the cork out with her beak and placed it in Dolores's hand.

"Thank you, Ixchel." Dolores tilted the glass heart, and the feathers floated out one by one, suspending themselves in the air. She motioned them gently into the palm of her hand.

La Chaquetza's eyes looked like they were going to pop out of their sockets, and she began to salivate. She hissed with her long lizard-like tongue and said, "Okay, my dear, hand them over to me like a good little girl."

Los Malalas also hissed loudly with excitement, and Los Chiquitos were frightened about what would happen next. They quickly gathered in a large clump and hugged each other for comfort.

Dolores walked over to La Chaquetza, looked into her cold-blooded eyes, and said, "First, you must let the little boy go."

La Chaquetza looked over at the boy and pointed at him. "That little boy? Do you mean El Oz? Why does he matter to you?"

Dolores said, "That little boy is El Oz?"

Pepito shook his head in disbelief and said, "That boy is El Oz? He's the one who is supposed to save us?" He slapped his forehead "Oh, boy! We're never going to get home."

Dolores looked at Necaxa for reassurance.

"Dolores, what are you going to do?" asked Necaxa.

"I was hoping you would tell me what to do," replied Dolores.

Necaxa took Dolores by the hand and said, "Dolores, do you remember when I told you that the answer lies within?"

Pepito said, "Why don't you just tell her how to follow her heart so we can get this all over with?"

Necaxa ignored Pepito and said, "Dolores, I told you at the beginning of your journey that you had to follow your heart. You would need to trust it. You were not listening to your heart when you believed that El Oz would be a man rather than a boy. You made up your mind about who he was before meeting him. Now, you are facing this difficult decision that affects each one of us standing before you, including you. You are now standing in the light of the truth. What will you do, Dolores?"

The crowd looked on with anticipation to see what Dolores would do next.

Dolores still needed reassurance. She looked toward the boy, who was exhausted and struggling to stand up from being tied up for so long. "Are you El Oz?"

He nodded.

She looked down at her chest and touched it with her hand, and then she used her finger to draw the shape of a heart. She looked up at Necaxa, who nodded in agreement. Dolores turned to La Chaquetza and said in a firm voice, "You will need to release El Oz first—and then I will give you the feathers." Dolores knew that El Oz was the only one who could help her return home.

"Dolores, please do not give her the feathers," El Oz said.

"I intend to keep my promise," replied Dolores.

La Chaquetza turned to Los Malalas. "Turn him loose!"

They hesitated.

"What are you waiting for? I told you to turn him loose!" shouted La Chaquetza.

One of Los Malalas stepped forward and said, "Do you promise not to leave us here?"

"Yes! I promise. Now, turn him loose!" shouted La Chaquetza.

El Oz said, "Do not give her the feathers."

Los Chiquitos said, "Don't give her the feathers!"

Dolores replied, "I intend to keep my promise to La Chaquetza, but she will have to let go of El Oz first."

"Do you intend to share the feathers with everyone?" Dolores asked. "Your sister, Necaxa, told me that when you were both young girls, you always dreamed of flying like the hummingbirds. She said a curandero gave you a potion that would help you grow wings, but now you can only fly short distances."

"Yes, my sweet little Dolores, that's true. My sister is trying to manipulate you. Do not be fooled by her. Now hand me those feathers like you said you would! You wouldn't want everyone here to think you lied to me, would you?"

"Shame on you, sister," said Necaxa. "Mother would so be ashamed of you. I am ashamed of you. You know that Dolores is going to keep her word by handing you the feathers because she has been taught that it is the right thing to do. But you have not fooled anyone—only yourself. Do you care what lies in store for each of us? Do you care whether you keep your word in front of everyone here, including your loyal servants, Los Malalas?"

One of Los Malalas stepped toward La Chaquetza and asked, "Are you going to betray us?"

La Chaquetza did not respond. It seemed like she would cry for a second, but she collected her emotions just as quickly as they set in.

Dolores walked over to where La Chaquetza stood.

Welo, Hierro, El Leon, and Pepito were not far behind.

Dolores held the feathers in her palm tightly, and she reached out to give them to La Chaquetza—and the feathers floated out once again.

La Chaquetza watched the feathers do a slow dance in the air, and she became entranced by their mysticism. She cupped the palm of her hand and loved the feathers to her other palm.

Everyone in the crowd gasped once again. Their whispers created an eerie humming sound.

La Chaquetza held the feathers tightly and waited for their magical powers to take effect. She paused and waited.

The crowd was in suspense because they knew that the wrath could begin at any moment, but nothing happened.

La Chaquetza made several attempts to fly, but she fell back to the ground. She was expecting her wings to lift her up, but the opposite happened. La Chaquetza gave Dolores a stern look and shouted, "You tricked me!"

"Sister, Dolores kept her promise. She gave you the feathers," exclaimed Necaxa.

"Yes, she did, but they don't work! Do they?"

"Dear sister, Dolores did precisely as she said she would. She gave you the feathers. Could it be that the feathers were not ever meant for you?"

La Chaquetza screamed, "You are going to pay for this! You will see. Everyone is going to pay!"

With their wings no longer giving them the ability to fly short distances, La Chaquetza and Los Malalas scurried through the canal bank and toward the horizon.

The crowd was left relieved by La Chaquetza's departure.

Dolores, Welo, Hierro, El Leon, and Pepito hugged one another.

El Oz said, "Let us go back to the village to rest. There is nothing more to do here."

15

THE TRANSFORMATION

El Empresario said, "Good morning. Who wants breakfast? Wake up, Welo, Hierro, and El Leon." He walked over to the casita where Dolores and Pepito were fast asleep. "Dolores! Pepito! It is time to wake up."

Dolores sat up in her bed, stretched her arms, and said, "Good morning, Welo."

She walked over to the window and saw hundreds of monarch butterflies sprinkled across the sky. They were much larger than the ones back home on her ranchito. She remembered the story her Tia Tonia told her. "Butterflies are little travelers guided by a higher purpose. They follow their hearts, which serve as an internal compass."

Dolores realized that there was a connection between her dilemma in trying to get home and the life mission of the butterfly. But what was it? She stared out the window and hugged herself for comfort. Her bare arms were rough and scaly. As she rubbed her arms, her skin fell off in tiny flakes. She was so alarmed she ran over to the bed where Pepito was fast asleep and burrowed in blankets. She pulled the covers up and immediately noticed Pepito had wings. She was terrified at the sight. She shook Pepito, and he finally woke up.

"Leave me alone. I'm tired," said Pepito in a gravelly voice.

"Pepito! Pepito! You have wings!" shouted Dolores.

"I know. I grew these things last night—and I took them for a spin around Ozlandia!" Pepito yawned, rolled over, and went back to sleep.

Welo, Hierro, and El Leon darted into the casita.

Welo asked, "What's all the commotion?"

"Pepito grew wings last night!" answered Dolores.

"Something fishy is going on here because El Leon lost all of his hair," said Hierro.

"I think we better go find El Oz," said El Empresario.

The group headed toward the plaza of Ozlandia, which was the center of the village, and saw the regular hustle and bustle of daily business activity. The day before, many of Los Chiquitos had stood in line at various puestos with destination signs. As they walked through the village, they were greeted by everyone.

Dolores overheard two Chiquitos whispering, "She is one brave little girl."

When they finally reached El Oz, they knocked on the door. The casita was empty except for the old rugs on the floor.

An older woman said, "Please come in. El Oz has been waiting for you."

Dolores greeted the woman and introduced everyone in the group.

El Oz was in the middle room with hundreds of lit candles.

His ankles were under his thighs, and his hands were extended. His eyes were closed, and he made a humming sound, which sounded like the speedy flapping of butterfly wings. He opened his eyes and asked the group to sit down. "What brings you here?"

Dolores said, "Well, as you know, I need to get back home to my ranchito. I miss my family terribly."

El Oz turned to Welo and asked, "Welo, how can I be of service to you?"

Welo cleared his throat nervously and said, "I am a community garden organizer. Our fruits and vegetables are no longer as robust each harvest season. La Chaquetza has been spraying poison in the fields. Los Chiquitos have become ill and are starving because they cannot grow food. Please help us. We don't have anyone else to turn to."

El Oz turned to Hierro and asked, "Welo, how can I be of service to you?"

"El Oz, I lost my mojo, and it has impacted the business of my recycling center. I tell lies to make Los Chiquitos believe I'm more successful than I am. Lying makes me feel bad inside. Do you think El Oz can help me?"

El Oz turned to El Leon and asked, "El Leon, how can I be of service to you?"

El Leon began to meow excessively. "Please help me! Meow! Meow! Meow! I was told that I was supposed to roar when I got older, but I never had anyone to show me how. I have no voice, and no one loves me. The ringmaster said I was too old to roar."

Dolores hugged El Leon and stroked his mane. She turned to El Oz and said, "Thank you! Thank you!"

"I feel better already. Meow! Meow! Meow!" said El Leon.

El Oz said, "My dear friends, let's all head to the plaza so I may present these new requests in the presence of Los Chiquitos."

When they arrived at the plaza, they walked into a festive affair with music, dancing, and laughing.

El Oz stood at the top of the ledge of the fountain centered within the plaza circle. "Gather around, everyone! I will present three gifts to our new dearest friends. Welo, Hierro, and El Leon who have conducted themselves nobly throughout their journey to Ozlandia, and their heroic efforts have benefitted us all. We are also going to send our dear Dolores and her beloved Pepito back to their family and ranchito."

Welo, Hierro, and El Leon stepped forward.

"Welo, Hierro, and El Leon, please hold your right hands and put your left hands on your hearts."

El Oz reached for Welo's hand, placed a hummingbird feather in his palm, and said, "Welo, I gift you this hummingbird feather. It will heal the Chiquitos and protect your community garden. You will never worry about La Chaquetza again." El Oz reached up for Hierro's hand and placed a hummingbird in his hand. "Hierro, I gift you this hummingbird feather. It will protect you and heal you from telling lies in the future. Remember, you are enough as you are." El Oz reached for El Leon's paw and placed a feather in it. "El Leon, I gift you this hummingbird feather. It will give you back your voice and your roar. I'm sorry, but this feather will not help you be loved. You will have to learn to love yourself first—and soon others will follow."

Dolores remembered her promise to Mr. Frog. "Wait! Mr. Frog

also had a request. He asked if you could remove La Chaquetza's spell."

"Dolores, each one of us here will transform, including Mr. Frog and all of his toad friends. When this happens, all will be forgiven—and all spells that have been cast will be eliminated. Each one of us will be free."

At that moment, a bolt of lightning sent all of Los Chiquitos scurrying for cover.

El Oz, Dolores, and Pepito stood their ground as La Chaquetza soared into where they stood.

"You need to make good on your promise," screamed La Chaquetza. "You gave me these useless feathers!"

El Leon now had more confidence and became annoyed with La Chaquetza's bullying. He let out a deafening roar that frightened La Chaquetza and Los Malalas.

Los Chiquitos all applauded El Leon's robust roar.

La Chaquetza cried out with frustration and almost lost her balance.

Welo ran toward her and caught her just as she was about to hit the ground. She quickly pushed him away and started weeping.

Los Malalas hissed and seemed confused. They had never seen weak behavior in their leader before.

Los Chiquitos looked at each other and started humming.

Dolores walked over to La Chaquetza, took her claw like hand, and hugged her. "I'm sorry you cannot fly."

La Chaquetza sobbed uncontrollably.

Hierro, El Leon, and Pepito walked over and stood behind

Dolores. Something felt different this time than in previous times. La Chaquetza was pitiful and defeated.

"I did exactly what you told me," said Dolores. "When Necaxa gave me the hummingbird feathers, she said to never let them go. Tia told me a story one day of the monarch butterfly and how they never get lost and always know their way home. They have an internal compass that directs them on which way to go, and Necaxa told me to follow my heart. That is what I did when I gave you the hummingbird feathers. I followed my heart."

Everyone in the plaza moved in closer to where Dolores was standing.

"We are all connected in some magical way. I cannot explain it, but I know in my heart that we will all find our way home." Dolores paused and looked at El Leon. "We have to love one another."

El Leon looked at Welo and pointed in the air. "We have to respect each other."

Welo looked at Hierro and cleared his throat. "Forgive." He looked at La Chaquetza and pointed at her. "We have to forgive her and Los Malalas."

Los Chiquitos made deafening humming noise and nodded.

Hierro looked at El Leon and said, "We have to be kind to one another. Dolores, you are the sweetest and kindest person I know."

La Chaquetza sobbed quietly and extended her hand to Dolores with an open palm that held the feathers. "So, you didn't trick me?"

"I told you the truth. I would never tell a lie to you or anyone else," replied Dolores.

La Chaquetza looked at Dolores, wept and said, "But the feathers do not work." A tear trickled down La Chaquetza's cheek and fell onto La Chaquetza's palm. When it landed on the feathers, she closed her hand and held the feathers tightly.

"There is something El Oz would like to share with you," Necaxa said.

El Oz stood on the ledge of the fountain and said, "La Chaquetza forgot who she was. Forgetting who you are and trying to become something else is dishonoring yourself. She thought that if she had the feathers, only she would be able to fly. Little did she know we were all meant to fly. Each of us was meant to soar! In times of uncertainty, we must not lose the sense of our character and the time we have right now. We were all created to experience peace and happiness in our lives. Dolores learned that he or she who brings peace holds the power. And for that, she is our queen of La Paz. Dolores was honorable in the way she forgave La Chaquetza. She forgave her for the misery she caused her and her loyal friends on her journey to Ozlandia. Just think, if each of us here in Ozlandia were to demonstrate for only one day the supreme virtues of love, faith, hope, mercy, and charity as Dolores has shown La Chaquetza, how we could collectively transform the land we live in. And we have." El Oz turned to La Chaquetza. "Forgetting where you came from is dishonoring who you are—and forgiveness is not a comfortable act. It asks us to transform into a higher version of ourselves.

Pepito shouted, "Well, I love everyone, but I don't love La Chaquetza for what she did. So, I don't forgive her!"

The crowd booed.

Pepito said, "I'm just kidding, okay." He jumped into the air, flapped his wings, and started to fly.

Ixchel flew in to join Pepito in the air, and they hovered over the group.

Dolores shouted, "Pepito, you are going to hurt yourself. Come down here at once!"

"I'm trying, but I can't," replied Pepito. "I guess this is my new normal. Oh, well."

El Oz's skin crackled, and two wings popped out of his back. They were beautifully shaped wings with orange and black colors and a red hint, just like the design in Dolores's China Poblana dress. El Oz turned into a beautiful monarch butterfly and took Dolores's hand. "Dolores, this is a big moment for you. You were always on your way home." He turned to the crowd. "Safe travels, everyone! Be sure to spread peace and love wherever you are and wherever you go." El Oz flew into the sky.

"Don't leave us! How will we find our way home?" Dolores asked.

El Oz was high in the sky, and they could barely see him. "Don't worry. Your internal compass will guide you. You're almost there, Dolores!"

Pepito flew down and stood next to Dolores. "We're already there? No, I don't think so. How can we be already there when we're still here!" He jumped into her arms and cried like a puppy.

Dolores lifted him up and kissed the top of his head. She turned to face the crowd with a look of defeat and disappointment. She cried softly and said, "Necaxa, I don't understand. This is all so confusing to me. I want to go home. I miss my family"

"Do not cry, little one." Necaxa motioned for La Chaquetza to approach. "Sister, I love you. Open your palm."

Weeping and remorseful, La Chaquetza followed her sister's command and watched the feathers as they slowly floated into the air just above their heads.

Necaxa said, "Dolores, you still have one more step before the feathers' powers can take effect. But first, say goodbye to your friends."

Dolores turned to Welo, Hierro, and El Leon and said, "I never really had friends before, but I do know for certain that you three have been the best friends I will ever have. I don't know what I could have done without each of you. I'll miss you and will always have you in my heart—no matter how far we are."

Pepito jumped out of Dolores's arms and hugged Welo, Hierro, and El Leon, and they all cried.

"Dolores, it's time to go home," said Necaxa. "La Chaquetza's tear activated the feathers, but we still have one more act to do quickly before the feathers fall to the ground."

Dolores held Pepito tightly in her arms and replied, "I'm ready."

"Dolores, step into the sunlight and twirl slowly," said Necaxa. "We will need each sparkle in your China Poblana dress to activate each of the hummingbird feathers."

Los Chiquitos hugged one another and waited for the feathers' mystical powers to take.

Dolores twirled slowly and saw the reflection of each sequin of her dress illuminating the feathers.

Pepito shouted to the crowd, "I love you all!"

Dolores and Pepito watched as Los Chiquitos and Los Malalas transformed into monarch butterflies and flew into the sky.

Ixchel guided them into the clouds and quickly flew back and landed on Dolores's shoulder.

It was Welo, Hierro, and El Leon's turn to travel home. They had become loyal friends, and now that they each had a hummingbird feather for protection, they would be able to transform their environments back home. They hugged one another, transformed into butterflies, and flew away.

La Chaquetza and Necaxa hugged and joined hands, and they turned into the most beautiful and regal monarch butterflies. They would now live harmoniously and help others do the same. They joined hands like the loving sisters they were always meant to be and flew into the sky.

Everyone was on their way home—except for Dolores and Pepito. Dolores looked at Pepito and said, "It looks like we're going to be home soon, Pepito."

Suddenly, Pepito's head sprouted antennae, and his tail shriveled up. His hair turned black, and his wings took color. Dolores's China Poblana wrapped around her waist and took the form of two large wings. They were both transformed into regal monarch butterflies.

Ixchel motioned for Dolores and Pepito to follow her, and they flew into the sky. They were finally on their way home.

16

A Return to El Ranchito

"Dolores! Dolores!"

Dolores heard the familiar voice of Tia Tonia. She also heard murmuring voices and struggled to open her eyes. There it was again: her Tia Tonia's voice.

"Wake up! Wake up! Dolores! Dolores! Are you all right?"

She could feel her body shake and heard her name called out again.

Dolores could hear Pepito barking, but she could not wake herself up completely. She tried to open her eyes once more, but she only caught glimpses of light and the shapes of four people. She felt Pepito licking her face and thought, *This feels like home.* She immediately came to her senses. She was surrounded by Tia Tonia and her tios: Welo, Pablo, and Leo.

Dolores was so excited to see the family. She was finally home and could hardly wait to tell her family about the incredible adventure she and Pepito took. She said, "Tia! Tios! I have been looking for you. I fell asleep, and it was very windy. It began to rain, and then I woke up in Ozlandia. Tia Tonia, we were lost. I was so scared. This place was beautiful and scary at the same time. Pepito and I became friends with the hummingbird. Her name was Ixchel. Tia Tonia, I do not know what I would have done without her. We were trying to find our way home for the longest time. We met a woman whose name was Necaxa. She became our protector. And do you know what? Pepito could even speak!"

Tia Tonia felt Dolores's forehead with the back of her hand and said, "My dear, you didn't go anywhere. You have been right here all along." She stroked Dolores's hair to comfort her and noticed a big lump on the back of her head. "Dolores, you must have hit your head really hard."

"Tia, I wasn't here. I was in Ozlandia. Pepito can now speak. He spoke there the whole time!"

Tia Tonia and the tios had never known Dolores to lie about anything. They thought that she must not be feeling well and looked at her with compassion.

"Pepito, show them you can speak," Dolores said.

Pepito barked loudly and threw flips.

Everyone chuckled at Pepito's peculiar behavior.

"Really, Tia, Pepito can speak! I don't know why he isn't speaking right now. And do you want to know something else, Tia Tonia? We also made three friends along the way. Welo, Hierro, and El Leon. They were all trying to find their way too, only in life and not necessarily trying to get home, like Pepito and me."

Tio Welo picked up Dolores, and they walked toward the ramada. The fierce winds had ripped the large bougainvillea off its roof and columns.

"We'll have a lot of cleaning up to do tomorrow morning," said Tio Hierro.

It was time for dinner. Tio Welo helped Dolores sit down at the dinner table.

Dolores looked at Tia Tonia and said, "Tia, why don't you believe me?"

Tia Tonia said, "Dolores, do you know what I believe? I believe that tree limb hit your head hard. The storm passed quickly, and you were only out there for no more than an hour. We were worried about you."

"Tia, there was this little boy they called El Oz. At first, I thought he was a wise old man, but it turned out he was only a little boy. Tia, he was about the same age as me."

Tia Tonia shook her head in disbelief. "Young lady, I'm going to make you a cup of tea de manzanilla. It will help to calm your nerves."

Dolores said, "Tio Leonardo, there was this beautiful lady who helped us. Her name was Necaxa. She gave me a red glass heart that held the hummingbird feathers. Her sister was La Chaquetza, a mean lizard-looking lady who tried to hurt us. She was desperate to take the feathers away from me. You see, I have them right here around my neck." Dolores removed the red glass heart.

Tio Hierro walked in closer to examine it. "Where did you get that? Something is moving inside of it!"

"I told you. Necaxa gave it to me." Dolores removed the cork and looked inside. "Pepito, it's Ixchel!"

Pepito barked excitedly, and Ixchel flew out and circled the family from above. It stopped to greet Pepito by landing on the tip of his nose, which made him look cross-eyed, and then perched on Dolores's finger.

Tia Tonia and the tios looked on in astonishment.

At that moment, they heard Señora Vicenta's burro braying in the distance.

The family gathered by the front gate just like the day before. Señora Vicenta shouted, "I'm here for the rent."

Tio Welo stepped outside the gate and said, "Señora Vicenta, we don't have the money. We are trying our best, but now the storm has our damaged crops. It will be extremely hard to make any money now. We need more time."

Dolores noticed a man walking toward them on the dirt road. As he approached, Dolores shouted, "Tia! Tia! It's Tio Ozvaldo!" She and Pepito took off running to meet him.

Pepito and Ixchel were not far behind.

When Tio Ozvaldo finally made it through the gate, he was met by his brothers.

Tia Tonia dropped to her knees in gratitude. Her prayers had been answered.

Tio Ozvaldo lifted Tia Tonia and said, "I missed you, Tia, and everyone so much. I was detained at the California border for several months. I am so sorry I did not write or send the money for the rent, but I saved all that I could. It's enough to buy the ranchito from Señora Vicenta."

Tia Tonia said, "Mijo, you are so thin. I'm going to serve you enough food that you won't be able to move."

The family laughed loudly through all their tears of joy because they knew Tia Tonia was serious.

Tio Ozvaldo walked over to Señora Vicenta, gave her a big hug, and handed her a satchel. "Señora Vicenta, here is the money for the ranchito plus interest. It is all I have. I am terribly sorry for all the inconvenience we have caused you."

There was complete silence. The family was finally free of the anxiety they had felt at the thought of being homeless—and they felt relief because they now had a permanent place to call home.

Señora Vicenta no longer had anyone to bully.

Dolores walked over, took her hand, and said, "Señora Vicenta, I forgive you."

Señora Vicenta burst into tears. The family quickly went in to console her. Ixchel landed on her hand. Welo helped her dismount from the burro. Dolores walked him into the yard of their ranchito and ran to get him a bucket of water. Pepito went to lick the leg of the burro. The burro returned the lick, almost knocking him to the ground.

Everyone congregated around the big table under the ramada.

"Who's hungry?" shouted Tia Tonia.

Before dinner, Tio Ozvaldo said, "During my time in the City of Angels, I had a lot of time to think about how we could improve our way of living. We are going to do something different this time. We're going to create a new business."

Señora Vicenta said, "Now that I'm no longer a landlord, I may be interested in investing in a good business with good people like you."

After dinner, Tio Welo ran into the house to get his accordion. Tio Hierro brought in an old tin bucket to use for a drum, and they both started playing a song.

Tia Tonia danced with Tio Ozvaldo.

Dolores twirled in her China Poblana dress and danced with Señora Vicenta.

Ixchel flew around the yard, sniffing all the plants and flowers, and Pepito jumped on the back of the burro and rode into the garden.

At that moment, thousands of monarch butterflies flew over the ranchito. Everyone admired their beautiful formations.

Dolores shouted, "Tia Tonia, look! They are following their hearts!"